Fade Away

(Fade Away, Book 1)

M. L. Newman

WILLIAM COLLINS

PUBLISHED BY:
William Collins Publishing, London

Copyright © 2015 by Ashley Newman
U.K., U.S.A., Canada

Editing services provided by LoriAnn Wale
Cover Design provided by Justin Janusaitis

More information can be found at the author's website http://mlnewmanauthor.com/

ISBN-13: 978-0692566602

ISBN-10: 0692566600

Table of Contents

Chapter One

"Fudge-o-lees," she said, wiping the royal purple paint from her ash blond hairline.

She grabbed two Q-tips and fixed the paint on her face the best she could. The rivaling colors of purple and yellow dazzled her hazel eyes. She had no worries of embarrassment as she grabbed her jacket and locked the dorm door. Tonight, she would be part of the sea of people doing the Wave and cheering for the undefeated Mountain Lions.

With her ticket in hand, she quickly made it across campus and inside the stadium before sprinting towards her roommates with the directions they had text messaged. She was almost awestruck at the great view. It was practically first row seating at the fifty-yard line.

"Lauren!" Gina yelled at her arrival.

"Told you I wouldn't be late."

"I was only kidding. Besides, we couldn't leave Taylor hanging tonight," Gina continued.

Lauren had barely sat down on the bleacher before the opposing team ran onto the field in their gold and black uniforms. The jeers and boos rang loudly from all around the stadium. If she listened hard enough, she was sure there was an echo, too. That all changed the instant the intercom introduced the Mountain Lions to the field.

She stood with the rest of the campus who wore the school colors or had painted their faces like she had, cheering and shouting in support. It wasn't until number thirty-four came into view that she really began to scream out. There was a difference in watching sports on the TV compared to being there live, and there was nothing else like it. The electricity of being part of the atmosphere was magical, and she couldn't believe how much she had missed, only starting to go to the games her senior year of high school. Of course, that was with a helpful push of a friend.

The game's outcome was painfully obvious in the third quarter. Unless the opposing team found a way to create ball movement to make at least three touchdowns, the fate of the game was already sealed. Taylor managed to tip the pass out of bounds close to the receiver, catching the football at the ten-yard line, sending ripples of excitement and roars throughout the stadium. Hilary high-fived everyone around as she bounced on the balls of her feet.

The Mountain Lions seemed to get a burst of energy realizing how close the other team came to scoring on their turf. The next play was cut short by a quick sack of the quarterback. In the following possession, the opposing team's quarterback threw the football up in a Hail Mary pass that spiraled almost perfectly towards the end zone when, out of nowhere, one of the Mountain Lions intercepted it, running as fast as he could while dodging other opponents to make the touchdown from down the field. Lauren almost lost her voice screaming out so loudly, watching her team win another game.

Lauren waited on the sidelines of the field while most of the crowd left to continue the celebration elsewhere. Gina, one of her roommates, was doing her best to be patient, but Lauren could read the excitement on her face of wanting to head back to the dorm. Her other roommate, Hilary, was completely oblivious as she and her boyfriend Tony kept rehashing the touchdown moments.

"Finally," Gina muttered.

Lauren looked across the field noticing the familiar figure headed over. Taylor, with his short blond hair that barely kissed his forehead, shone in the football field lights. She knew his eyes—the darkest brown eyes she'd ever known—were filled with excitement from the game even though she wasn't able to see them at the moment. The contrast between his dark eyes and light hair had struck her initially back when they were in middle school. He had been tall even then; but his height and muscles only grew with the years. He was one of the best defensive linebackers on the team now, but she knew the secret behind the aggression that improved his abilities on the field.

As he approached, Hilary grabbed Gina by the arm excitedly. Lauren was out of reach, but she knew what was coming. Hilary jumped right into her famous touchdown dance, which was forced upon them. Lauren laughed as even Tony joined in until Taylor reached them and joined in, too.

"Congrats, man," Tony greeted.

"Thanks," Taylor replied, picking up his duffle bag. "Party time?"

"Yes!" Gina cheered along with Hilary.

"Where is it? I wanna drop off my bag. I can meet you there," Taylor asked.

"Rodman building. Collin's room," Tony advised.

"Awesome. I'll see you guys there in a few."

They all began to walk towards the exit when Lauren noticed Taylor nodding her over. She joined his side as they split off into the direction of his room. His hair was still slightly damp from the quick shower after the game. As the brisk air seeped in, she tugged up the collar of her jacket. The minor dance break had warmed her marginally, but now that that was done, she needed to make a move into the warmth of a building.

"You're quiet tonight."

"Nothing a beer can't fix," he chuckled.

"Can we make a pit stop so I can wash my face?"

Taylor laughed. "There'll be plenty of people wearing their face paint. Don't be so self-conscious."

"I'm not," she muttered.

They walked the few blocks until his dorm appeared. His room was on the top floor, which was inconvenient, but his roommate spent most of the time at his girlfriend's off campus apartment. Most of the time, Taylor had the entire room to himself, as long as Jeff wasn't fighting with his girlfriend. Four flights of stairs later, he slid his key into the door only to throw the duffle bag haphazardly inside. She could already hear the story in the morning of how he tripped over it trying to get into bed, wasted.

Lauren spotted the bathroom as they walked down the hall but found herself caught up by the sleeve. Taylor tugged her past it towards the stairwell as she complained helplessly.

"Seriously?"

"Just leave it," he said.

"You're not giving me much of a choice."

He smirked as they finally reached the first floor and exited the dorm.

"I don't care what you say. I'm washing it off once we're there," she pouted.

He grabbed her chin forcefully, compelling her to stare into the darkness of his eyes. "Don't pout. It takes away from the beauty of your face."

Lauren smirked the best she could considering the grip he had on her. "Thanks. You did well tonight."

He let go with a shrug not bothering to comment. She knew that he wouldn't anyway.

They walked in the direction of the party, passing by the few academic buildings. It wasn't until they crossed the main road that she started to feel a tingle of unease. Lauren glanced back but saw nothing out of place. Shrugging, she continued to walk beside her friend who clearly hadn't noticed anything. Was the chill in the air setting off her mental alarms?

She should have been used to the cold weather, having spent her entire life in Minnesota. Had she not received a full scholarship to the state college, she would have moved down south already. There was no way she could throw away that type of opportunity, though. And having Taylor at the same school was a support that she appreciated.

The Rodman building stood ahead with lights shining from almost every window. Collin's room was on the first floor with the benefit that nobody complained about the noise. He constantly threw parties and drank into the early morning with no repercussions. It didn't hurt that he was perfect eye candy, so he generally got away with all sorts of things, although only a few girls were his type to get close enough for a taste of his charms.

The light posts just barely illuminated every few feet near the recycle bins and benches. She wouldn't have noticed the tall figure at all other than it was headed in their direction, coming opposite along the pathway. Taylor stepped towards the side out of the way, allowing room for the stranger to pass by.

A peculiar sound followed by a shout caused Lauren to scan the pathway around her. It was then that she realized Taylor was suddenly no longer with her. Even the tall figure who had just been there was missing. How bizarre.

"Taylor?"

Abruptly, a hand clasped around her throat, shoving her backwards off of the pathway into the darkness. There was no possible way for her to make a noise with the quickness of the movement. Just as fast as she had been shoved, her head was roughly pulled back with a violent tug of her hair, and warmth covered her mouth. It was then that she heard a rumble coming from within the hard chest before her. Lauren instinctively opened her mouth to scream when the stranger's tongue swiftly dipped inside.

She tried to shove the figure off, but she wasn't strong enough. That's when the grip around her throat tightened significantly. A rough scrape against her tongue forced tears out of her eyes as a new, warmer liquid began to fill her mouth. With her head tipped back and oxygen becoming a severe concern, the liquid slid down her throat inescapably.

"Lauren!" Taylor shouted.

It was so dark that she couldn't see her friend but instead heard his fast approach. She was clutched so tightly to whomever had her that her feet barely even touched the grass. The hand around her throat shoved her back as the stranger spun on Taylor with a growl.

Lauren clutched her neck as she doubled over trying to spit up what she had swallowed. She coughed as hard as she could until Taylor collided with her, sending them both to the ground. Taylor was only down for a second before he charged after the attacker. That's when she felt dampness on her shirt but couldn't see what it was. What kind of psychopath were they dealing with?

Taylor was fighting with the figure, throwing punches, but he was barely making any contact at all. She knew he was tired from the football game, but even that couldn't explain half of what she saw. The stranger moved like a shadow, and Taylor was the candlelight, never making contact with the attacker as he moved. There was no way someone could move so fast.

The figure's chest rumbled again, focused on Taylor, just like it had prior to attacking Lauren. She wasn't fit enough to take on a physical altercation, let alone an altercation with someone whom even Taylor couldn't take down. There was the only one logical action she could take. She finally found her voice and screamed as loudly as she could manage.

Three more students came running down the path to her surprise. Maybe there was a chance they could all take it down. The figure noticed the growing attention and took off into the darkness of the night. She glanced at Taylor as he held the side of his shoulder, looking after the figure's escape route.

"Taylor?"

His eyes took her in with a wince. "What the hell was that?"

"Did it hurt you?"

He pulled back his blood-covered hand as confirmation sunk in.

"We need to get help," she encouraged.

*****

Hours later, she was in her pajamas lying in bed, wrapped up in blankets with bruises around her throat and an endless mental rerun of the assault going through her head. Her still damp clothes were draped over the laundry bin. It was harder than she realized trying to get Taylor's dried blood removed. She had surpassed exhaustion what felt like years ago, yet her body refused to allow her to calm down and relax fully. Every bump or laugh she heard through the wall sat her straight up in bed, not that she was exactly lying down.

Taylor, on the other hand, had passed out right away. With his shoulder stitched up neatly and pain medication in his system from their visit to the hospital, there was little chance he'd have trouble sleeping. He had asked her if she wanted to sleep in his room, but she declined. She didn't want to admit out loud that even *his* muscles hadn't saved them, and while she held no grudge against him, his status as protector had been tarnished.

While calling her parents was the one thing she wanted to do all night, it was pointless now. It was so late (or early in the morning) that waking them up to worry over something that couldn't be changed was selfish. She knew her parents would have come up right away to see her, and they deserved at least one last night of good sleep before they found out. Even if sleep wouldn't come for herself.

The anxiety medication prescribed from the hospital merely numbed her emotions. It had all happened so swiftly that the only confirmation that it had happened at all was the bottle of pills and wristband still clinging to her. Taylor was sewn up and tended to while she tried to explain what happened to the nurse and doctor. The hospital called the police to report the incident.

Both the city police and campus police said that they would look into the attack, but she had no real description to give. It had happened so fast and it was so dark out that a description other than "the guy was tall" was a cruel joke. And the students who had come running to help were just as useless. All they had heard was her screaming; they hadn't seen anything out of place.

Lauren awoke late in the morning with her body tingling. Her adrenaline was easily spooked. She slid out of bed carefully so as not to wake Hilary. Gina was nowhere to be seen; maybe she'd spent the night with her boyfriend, Max. Grabbing a change of clothes, Lauren rushed into the shower room. She scrubbed anxiously around her mouth trying to suppress the memories from the night's misfortune before brushing her teeth just as vigorously.

Rather than waiting for the uneasiness to overtake her

emotions, she took a couple of pills and let her hair down, arranging it carefully around her neck, to dissuade conversation from others. She was already feeling self-conscious and didn't want to explain to anyone how she received the bruises. She grabbed her jacket as she went out the door with one destination in mind. The breeze was warmer than the previous night, but it still felt wrong. To be honest, nothing was feeling quite right; nonetheless, she pushed her discomfort into the back of her mind. Her muscles seemed to be extra sore, her mind slightly foggy, but she knew the welcoming numbness from the tablets would soon follow.

Luckily, someone was coming out of the slate-colored building as she was trying to go inside. The dorm was its usual calm self. She suspected the majority of the occupants were nursing hangovers from the festivities the night before. She made her way up to the top floor without even huffing a little, which amazed her. Clearly, the times she'd spent going up and down them had finally caused her body to be fit enough to handle it. She smiled at that thought as she raised her hand to knock. Her knuckles barely made contact with the door before it swung open with Taylor on the other side.

His hair was disheveled, and his eyes were somewhat unfocused. It appeared as though he was breathing heavily although his body barely moved. His fingers curled around the edge of the door before stepping back, allowing her entry. No sooner had she passed through the doorway that the door was shut and locked.

Lauren took in the room, noticing the blinds pulled down and closed while his bed was a mess with sheets tumbling to the floor. The bottle of pain medication sat on his desk next to his laptop. She looked back only to find Taylor resting his head against the door with his hands clenched in fists.

"Are you okay?"

"Not really," he said.

"Do you need more meds?" she asked, grabbing his bottle, which was already half-empty. "Did you take all those last night?"

"It's not enough. I need something stronger," he commented.

"It takes the edge off, though."

"Maybe for you..."

She went over to his side. "Do you want me to check it?"

He shook his head at first until he turned to look at her. "Okay."

Lauren patted his arm, encouraging him to sit on the bed. She grabbed the gauze from the table to change his bandage. He grit his teeth as he sat with his hands still clenched tightly.

"I'll be gentle," she said softly as she began to unpeel the wrappings covering his shoulder.

There was no way to be prepared for the sight before her. The wound was much worse than she believed it was last night. It had been stitched back together after the savage assault; however, it still screamed for attention. It was almost like the stitches were keeping the petals of a flower from blooming. No wonder he was in pain. She couldn't understand why he didn't receive something more substantial for medication, but she was no doctor. She wrapped his shoulder with fresh gauze after cleaning it as tenderly as possible.

When she was finished, he thanked her gratefully. Their friendship had always been an independent dependence where he claimed to not need help when it was offered only to concede later. He had his reasons for why he kept his distance, and she respected his boundaries, which had blossomed their friendship. She knew why she was kept at arm's length, but the mere fact that he accepted her into his inner circle meant a great deal.

Taylor was more than just easy on the eyes, as any football player with great looks was. The difference was he never chased after females. They practically tripped all over themselves to be near him, and yet he barely acknowledged them, other than to sleep with them. He knew they were looking for more, and he couldn't provide it. Maybe "couldn't" was too strong a word; "wouldn't" was a bit more accurate. Instead, he'd tell women up front whether he was interested or not. Lauren could only imagine where the conversation went from there, but she was the longest relationship he'd ever known. Friendship and romance combined. It was safe.

"Have you eaten?"
"No. You?" he asked.
"No, but we should. I can order pizza."
"Go for it," he encouraged.

She took out her phone and completed the task in minutes. As she began to put her phone away, a message came across the screen from her mom.

Going to get a manicure. A new place the next time you're home. I love you!

Lauren smirked at the message until she remembered she was going home next weekend. There was no way that she'd be able to hide the bruises, and she really needed to tell them, right?

"I'm supposed to do the laundry trip home next weekend."

"Do mine too, will ya?" he asked.

"No way," she said, sitting in his desk chair. "Mom is gonna flip about this."

"You're telling her?"

"There's no way to hide this," she said, gesturing to her darkly bruised neck.

Taylor frowned deeply for a few minutes before waving her over. "Let's see what we're dealing with."

Lauren wanted to refuse again, regardless of the intimidating look he was expressing; it wouldn't change that she couldn't hide the marks. She knew it wouldn't look worse than his injury, but it was still stressing her out. If she wasn't down to the last of her clean clothes, she could put off the visit for another week at least.

Once sitting beside him on the bedside, his fingers began to push her hair behind her shoulders. She closed her eyes as he leaned in to get a closer look. Sharply, he sucked in a deep breath causing her eyes to flick to his.

"What?"

"I... it's... wow," he commented.

"Taylor..."

"It's just not possible."

"You're freaking me out!" she yelled.

His hands gripped her biceps. "The marks aren't... they're fading."

"It just happened last night, and it's healing?"

"No, Lauren, it's fading away."

She jumped up from the bed, rushing over to the standard full-length mirror that came in every room. She shoved her hair back to inspect her neck and lost her breath completely. The dark bruises, that she was certain were there this morning, were only a light shade of purple. She couldn't tell what was going on, but it wasn't normal. None of it was.

Chapter Two

By Thursday, Lauren was so confused by the attack that parts of it were beginning to fade just like the bruises. Any worries she had about telling her parents over the coming weekend had dissipated. There wasn't anything to see, and she wasn't sure how to explain it if she had to.

Gina had spent the entire weekend of the attack with Max and during the week had been shuffling from class to class. Lauren had barely seen her, which helped having to explain her awkward silence. Hilary spent more time in the dorm room, which caused her to be more careful. The tension was clear in her body language just being around Hilary.

Classes were preparing for midterms, which helped her focus completely. It wasn't new material that she had to cram in, and she made sure to spend time organizing her notes, highlighting important passages and listening to the professor. A few of them were cryptic enough to drop exam hints in between the lessons that only a few people caught. She highlighted anything repeated more than once.

It was approaching late afternoon, and she had a half-hour to consume anything somewhat quickly. She stopped into the closest deli, grabbing a chicken Caesar salad and settling into one of the corner seats. While her day had been vaguely stressful, it was refreshing to be surging on a project or two.

Her night class, Historic Theatre, was in her favorite building with the cutest professor on campus. Professor Klein had been in more than a few of her daydreams with his sandy brown hair and cute dimples. Every time he called on her in class, her skin would rise in goose bumps. He was easily in his early thirties, but his spirit didn't know it. He was down to earth, bridging the gap from centuries long gone to the present.

While Professor Klein was the perfect specimen of a man in her mind, he was the best distraction. He was completely unattainable, just the way she liked it. Her last relationship had ended with her sobbing into a pint of ice cream while her ex was busy taking out a girl he met in one of his courses. He hadn't admitted to cheating on her, but she could see the spark in his eyes when he talked about breaking up. That spark never appeared once through their three months together.

Lauren sipped her water, rolling her eyes at the thought. Professor Klein was the perfect distraction, and she'd take his smile any day. With that in mind, she tossed her barely touched salad and left the deli, zipping up her jacket as she went. The chill in the air had picked up during the week causing most students to scurry quickly from one building to another.

She walked through the grand archway inside the building, down the staircase to the basement level and down the hall into the last room on the left. The lights were dim and the projector was down, which lightened her mood even more. It was a movie day. She tossed her backpack down in the seat beside her and tugged out her notebook.

Her fascination with art history started at a young age when her class took a tour to the museum in the city. The statues of important people from far off places had encouraged her to take a deeper interest in history. There was no chance to learn art without the history, and she relished the knowledge.

"Ms. Benson, today you beat even me."

Lauren smiled brightly. "It was chilly today."

"Yes, yes, I know. Winter will be brutal this year. I can feel it."

She nodded an agreement as he walked to the front of the room, placing down his messenger bag. He pulled out a few items, setting up while her peers trickled in little by little. Professor Klein appeared at ease in his white button up shirt and a burgundy tie.

Fallon sat in the chair opposite Lauren's backpack. She kept to herself for the most part. Her dark brown hair was a shield to keep others out, presumably. The most Lauren had managed to get from her was a nod of acknowledgment. Nothing more, nothing less.

The class kept to schedule with a short explanation of what they were going to watch before he put on the movie. It was a black and white film that clearly turned off some students right away. She, however, leaned her head against her propped up hand and watched the movie with interest. The characters in theatre were hardly ever pure all the way through except for maybe one. That thought had kept her mindlessly guessing which one would do the other in until she heard coughing from Fallon.

Lauren glanced over as Fallon coughed and coughed until she grabbed her bag and left the room. No one seemed bothered in the least, but Lauren felt nervous. What if she needed help? Without thinking it through completely, she grabbed her bag and followed Fallon's trail out of the room. The hallway was empty, but she could still hear her coughing through the door of the women's bathroom.

"Hey, are you okay?" Lauren asked once inside.

Fallon's light green eyes squinted impossibly tight as she coughed even more. She fumbled around in her bag until she pulled out a small white inhaler. Lauren had no idea that the girl was asthmatic, but it comforted her to know that she had attempted to help her. That comfort slid away, though, when their eyes met again.

"Stay away from me."

Confusion distorted Lauren's features. "I just wanted to check on you."

"I'll be safer once you're gone."

"Wait. What?" she asked, even more confused.

Fallon grabbed her bag and slid it onto her shoulder with agitation. "Check the back of your hands."

Lauren looked down hurriedly, turning her hands over, and realized the awfulness of it all. Her veins were no longer a bluish tint raised up in her skin. They were now an unmistakable black. And it didn't stop there—veins running through the palms of her hands and wrists appeared the same dark hue.

"I don't understand," she said, although it was obvious

something was clearly wrong.

Fallon glared as she began trying to walk around her at a distance in the small room. "Keep telling yourself that. Just don't bite me."

"Why would I do that?"

"Because..." Fallon's words stopped as she looked up at her.

"Because *what*?" Lauren questioned further.

Fallon shook her head. "I'm not getting involved in this. Good luck."

Lauren watched her reach for the door. "Good luck?"

"That you don't turn into one of them."

With that response, she disappeared out of the door in the opposite direction of the classroom. Lauren stood with her jaw slack. What was Fallon talking about? Turn into what? She hadn't exactly felt normal since the attack, but what else was expected? Was she nervous to walk alone at night? Of course, she was, but so was every other person who dealt with an attack. Maybe she needed to check in with Taylor.

She felt too uneasy to go back into the classroom, especially with the new development. Instead, she made her way back out of the building. Thursday was designated gym time for Taylor, and she knew he would be getting out relatively soon. She knew the strange fading effect of her wounds wasn't just happening to her. His shoulder was making such progress that his exercise schedule had no need to change.

Her stride took off at a good pace towards her destination, and with every step, her pulse thumped a little harder in her chest. The campus was falling into the lull of the evening. Students were either in the cafeteria having dinner, studying in their rooms or in night class. Where she was supposed to be. She shook her head and continued walking, but that overwhelming unease wouldn't stop causing tension in her shoulders.

Her eyes scanned her surroundings as she gripped her backpack straps. The large shadows from the trees only caused further anxiety since she knew how easy it would be for anything to hide there. It was then that she noticed the dorm in front of her and heard the all-too-familiar rumble from close proximity.

Instinct told her to run. It also told her to scream, not that she could. Her body had practically seized up with fear. Still, her legs kept pushing forward as though no threat had set off the internal alarm within her. With every step, another tingle coursed its way from her body to her brain. Her breath was composed as she reached for the handle of the door when her backside caught on fire and pressure squeezed her shoulder.

Lauren spun as fast as she could to face the attacker with her teeth grit between fear and violence. It was a shock to see Taylor before her, raising his eyebrow at her reaction. He was covered in sweat that shone on his skin from the light coming from the lamppost outside the door. She took a deep breath, trying to calm her insides with the relief that it was her friend who was near, but she was too hyped up to feel any change.

"Sorry, I was coming to see you," she said.

"Didn't mean to scare you. Come on."

She followed him inside where he buzzed them into the stairwell up to his room. When he opened the door and turned on the light, something struck her as odd. She took in his messy bed (which was normal), his desk, which had the usual laptop and notebook pending some assignment, but it wasn't that area that was unusual. When her eyes scanned to the other side of the room, it struck her—the bedding was gone, and all of Taylor's roommate's belongings were missing.

"Jeff moved off campus with his girlfriend," Taylor explained.

"That's pretty cool. Are they setting you up with someone else?"

"Nope, I've got this to myself until next semester." He smirked while grabbing a change of clothes and towel. "I'll be back."

Lauren nodded as he took off to the showers. Just as the door shut, the breeze from the movement rattled the full-length mirror. She went over to it, tugging back her hair to view her neck, but the discoloration was even fainter. Lauren looked down at her hands again. The black veins staring back at her were faint against her skin. How did Fallon even see this? Unless she was already aware...

With that thought in mind, she attacked Taylor's laptop. She pulled up the Internet search engine scouring for reports about attacks against people. A bunch of things about cannibals came up, which she wasn't looking for exactly. As she dug deeper into the search results, there were explanations of biting during sexual encounters, baby teething and animal attacks, but nothing that fit her description. Finally exhausted by it all, she searched for the report that she made with the police to find nothing at all. Not even a small article to warn others about what had happened to them. What the hell?

Her eyes were burning with frustration. Before she completely lost it, she scoured the school website for announcements from campus security. There was a warning about making sure to not leave the security door propped open, and making sure to turn the volume down by a certain time. Nothing was written about the attack or even to be wary about stranger danger.

She gripped her fists and heard a sound that scared her more than anything else. It was that ominous rumble, but as she scanned the room, she realized she was alone. Panic began to build as she checked the room two more times from her seat, terrified of someone attacking her at any moment. That's when she realized that she truly was alone, the rumble was coming *from her!* It was coming from her. Maybe Fallon was right to be afraid of her? What was wrong with her? As much as she wanted to ask her classmate more questions, she feared that she'd never see her again.

Taylor walked into the room with the smell of his body wash wafting around him. He was her best friend, and he had been attacked, too. He put his dirty clothes in the laundry basket and sat on the edge of the bed. Lauren felt her stomach tighten as she slid her hands into the sleeves of her hoodie.

"What's with you tonight?" he asked, running a hand over his shoulder.

Lauren couldn't take her eyes away from his actions. "Do you feel weird?"

"Weird? No," he replied.

A strange pull tugged within her, drawing her to stand before him. "Let me..."

She used her palm to encourage his head to lean away as she peered down at the fading wound. The skin that once appeared so angry was now calm with four tiny scars, like ripples on a pond. The stitches had detached days before in one long gentle pull, Taylor had explained over the phone. It was a strange sight watching something fade instead of scab over. She ran two fingers over her own throat, lost in fascination.

"Lauren?"

"Yeah?" she replied.

"What are you doing?"

"You're fading away, too. Faster than me," she said.

"All right, what's going on?" he asked, sitting back to look into her eyes. "You're acting all trippy."

She shook her head in disagreement while taking a step back. If she were acting strange, it would seem logical for Taylor to be as well, but he wasn't. He was perfectly normal. Perfectly perfect. It was probably her thoughts running away from her. Fallon had scared her; that's why she was reacting this way. It made sense.

"I decided to skip class tonight, but when I was walking, I got scared. So I came here."

"Historical theatre? You love that class," he said.

"That's beside the point."

"Come here," he said, gesturing for her to sit beside him. "You have every right to be scared. I can walk you from your evening courses if you'd like. I wouldn't mind."

"I'll be okay. Besides, you have football practice. I won't be the reason we lose games."

"I'd believe you if you hadn't randomly showed up tonight, acting weird. Don't worry about it," he said, making it easy.

She eyed him, not pushing him further. He was being extra nice, and while she didn't want to force him to watch over her, it was comforting. It was a special part of him that she saw rarely. Taylor hadn't asked for more than companionship, trust and loyalty. She could easily give that to him. He respected her choices and encouraged her whenever possible.

They spent the next hour watching mind-numbing TV in contented silence. Every once in a while, she could feel his dark eyes upon her. Had she not grown used to it over the years, it would have been uncomfortable. She focused her attention on the TV as a catchy insurance commercial played, allowing him to take his time. Of all the habits he'd displayed over the years, this was much more acceptable.

Lauren could tell by the desolate look upon his face that something was wrong. His eyes were glazed over and empty. When she offered him his favorite snack of chocolate pudding and he refused to acknowledge it on his desk, her worry deepened. He hadn't spoken all day, and even the teachers didn't look his way. She couldn't understand the severity of his mood.

Taylor had always been moody, perpetually swinging between cold encounters to calm acceptance. The quieter he was, the worse, in her opinion.

After the bell rang, she grabbed her backpack and went to her locker to discard the unneeded items for the evening. She made her way to the side stairwell, down and out to wait for Taylor at the stop sign as per usual. Strangely, he wasn't there yet. He always beat her to the stop sign, but not today. She only managed to spot him by his neon green designer sneakers, but he was a block up the street already. He'd left her? They'd walked together for the last few months like clockwork.

Lauren ran to catch up to him, but he didn't even notice. She wanted to ask him what was wrong but didn't want to anger him. Instead, she walked in silence beside him the next few blocks until she turned onto her street. At the corner, her pace slowed down, and to her surprise, so did his.

"Taylor?" she asked.

When he turned to look at her, his expression was of the coldest demeanor that scared her silent again. The last thing she wanted was to make him angry, so she said nothing and waved goodbye to him. The rest of the walk home, she felt uncomfortable and restless. Even watching TV with her dad couldn't settle her insides. What could she do to help her friend?

The next day at school was worse. Her friend was gone, but his body remained. Still he kept his silence, even with her. And again, after school ended, he'd walked off before she'd arrived at the stop sign. Lauren caught up to him like the day before, and in the same manner, he slowed just before she turned onto her own street. Unlike the previous day, she kept her mouth shut, although her eyes were filled with so many questions. His dark eyes glanced her way, daring her to ask even one, but she only waved farewell.

It went on for weeks, just the same. She adjusted to needing fewer items and not stopping at her locker at the end of the day.

Lauren's eyes glimpsed the time. "I've got to get back."

"Why not crash here?"

"There's no bedding. I have homework I need to finish—"

"Such a girl. I have extra sheets you can use and then wash when you go home this weekend," he smirked.

"You are awful."

"And you know it. Are you seriously going to make me walk you to your dorm? I might just crash in your room then," he said.

With midterms coming up, that would be a cramp in Hilary's studying habit. It would be rude, and while she did want to go back to the comfort of her own room, not walking the campus at night was curbing her choice. There was a free bed available here, and she wouldn't have to worry about Jeff coming back. She nodded in agreement, and they set to work, Lysol-spraying the mattress and putting on fresh sheets and a blanket, all the while trying to keep her hands tucked into the sleeves of her hoodie. Taylor gave her one of his pillows to use, and she was all set.

"Thanks for letting me stay."

"It was your plan all along," he teased.

"Oh, yeah, I wanted to get stuck doing your laundry this weekend."

Taylor only laughed, not bothering to comment.

*****

She only had one course for the day, but it began at eight in the morning. It was awful having to get up, but it was a great feeling knowing she was done for the week. Lauren had kept her word and stripped the bed, putting the sheets in his duffle, which she carried back to her dorm in the morning. Even as quietly as she tiptoed, he had sat up to check on her.

Her class was going to start soon, so with little choice, she chucked the duffle on her bed and hightailed it to class. Luckily, the class was reflecting on the chapter assigned from Wednesday, and she participated accordingly. And just like a speeding rocket, she was soon in her dorm room packing up what she needed to bring home.

"So..."

Lauren looked up into the curious eyes of Hilary. "What?"

"You're not one to spend the night prowling. What were you up to?"

"Prowling?" She laughed hesitantly. "Taylor and I watched movies until late. His roommate moved off campus, so I crashed there."

"Where's the fun in that?" she complained. "I demand a juicy story!"

"Maybe Gina will have one."

"Come on, Lauren, I'm living vicariously through you. There's so many cute guys here," Hilary pushed.

"And how does Tony feel about that?" Lauren teased back while checking that she had everything she needed.

Hilary laughed loudly. "He's the reason I'm asking. Guess who's interested!"

Lauren ignored her, searching through her purse for the keys to her car. This wasn't the first time she and Tony had played matchmaker. For as long as they had been roommates, she'd been shoved in every male's direction until Quinn. She bit her tongue at the thought.

"I know you want to know," Hilary continued. "Believe it or not, even I was surprised. But he was the one to ask Tony about you."

Lauren grabbed the duffle off the bed, slung her purse on her shoulder and grabbed the handle of her own laundry basket. It wasn't a good idea to let Hilary get the hint that she was listening. She knew every relationship enhanced her best qualities, learning from the mistakes and growing, but she wasn't sure she had truly healed from the break up with Quinn. Instead, she made her way to the door, tugging it open with her free hand.

Hilary, noticing that she wasn't slowing down, came up from behind her. "Collin was really bummed you no-showed."

Every hair on Lauren's head stood on end at the name drop. There was no way that she heard that right. She blinked a few times while anticipating her foot to continue out the door.

"So can Tony give him your number? He wants to set something up," Hilary mentioned.

"He's not interested in me. We just have night class together," she said.

Lauren had been so focused on the little things like Professor Klein, Fallon, everything except for the fact that they shared that class. Collin sat on the opposite side of the room and barely spoke to her, although she didn't really give him a chance when she was so focused on her coursework and professor. Fudge-o-lees.

"So you wouldn't care if he called you then?"

"He won't call me, but go ahead. It'll get you and Tony off of my back."

Hilary responded with a small laugh. "Enjoy your weekend, Lauren."

Chapter Three

Lauren had barely a minute to set down her bags when her mom, Claire, whirled in like the fabulous tornado she was. Her mom was always stylish when she dressed for the day, even on the weekends. While she had grown up following in her mother's footsteps, she lost the excitement of being fashionable, especially when she was the one who had to pay the bill. Much to her father's relief, at least her tops were always respectably nice even paired up with slacks, skirts or jeans.

Her mom was grabbing her purse with keys in hand, headed for the door, only to stop short at her presence. Her mom's green eyes lit up along with her smile, as she tugged Lauren into a hug.

"I'm so glad you're here! I was going to shop a bit."

"Okay, let me throw my stuff in my room," Lauren replied.

It took her a few minutes while her mom started the car. As she dropped off the belongings in the familiar room, she sighed, noticing the boy band poster of Links & Chains still hanging on the wall and the light blue walls with clouds and stars on the ceiling. The many pillows stacked up on the cream-colored bedding teased her to come lie down for a nap, but she couldn't. She shut the door and made her way out of the house and into the awaiting vehicle.

"How are things at school?"

Lauren mindlessly watched the small suburban town pass by in a blur as her mother drove. The ground level community center building sat across from the white-colored town hall building. She'd spent summers volunteering at the community center through high school to assist her college application activity list. "Good. Really good.

I like my courses this semester."

"That's good. And how are the girls doing?"

"They're fine. Gina has been busy, so I haven't seen her other than the football games. Hilary is the same as ever," Lauren commented, rolling her eyes.

Claire chuckled. "At least you have them. I've heard horror stories about impossible roommates. Especially at your age."

"I know. How are things at home?"

"Well, you know your father is as bad as you when it comes to football. I have to read on the other side of the house with headphones on, or I'll hear him hollering down the house. He's happy, though, so I wouldn't begrudge him that. Work is a bit stressful, so we allow each other space for enjoyment."

"Enjoyment?" Lauren asked.

"Shopping," her mom said with a smile.

"How's the office?"

She could tell by the grip her mom had on the steering wheel that she'd taken a misstep. Her mom was trying to get a promotion that was well overdue and deserved, but no one had realized that the boss's nephew was going to join the department. Even though he was new, he knew the business well, but nothing compared to what her mom could accomplish. It was a sore subject.

"Sorry, mom," she said.

"It's perfectly acceptable for you to ask. I only wish I had some good news to share. At this point, the nepotism is so glaringly obvious that it looks like neither of us will get the position"

Lauren shook her head but wouldn't comment. Better to leave

that discussion for another time. Luckily, the shopping center wasn't too far away. The cluster of shopping opportunities ranged from an organic grocery to the sporting goods store, with clothing shops and a beauty salon in between. It wasn't usually that crowded on the weekends, but with the holidays coming, people were making their rounds early this year. The shoe store was their first stop.

Her mom was a shoe slayer—a term she had proudly come up with on her own. Somehow, her shoes never lasted more than a season, which didn't bother her. She was always on the ready, buying more, but it was the strangest thing Lauren had ever known. It wasn't that her mom was rough on them or at least not that Lauren could tell. It seemed her luck with shoes was forever stuck on bad. It was a tradition for them to always begin with the shoe department, laughing over which shoe had lost a heel first or disappeared completely.

While her mom scanned the options, Lauren ventured over to the boot section. Her taste was stuck between very conservative and slightly edgy. There was no explanation how her tastes ranged easily from a pair of peep toe to converse-styled high heels. Even her mom couldn't get it. Maybe underneath it all, she was more daring now that Hilary and her fashion influence had helped to evoke it.

The thought of Hilary only seemed to frustrate her further. There was plenty of time to find love and all the mushy stuff that went along with it. Why was she being pushed so heavily toward every male on campus? She was perfectly fine the way she was. She had two great roommates for support; she was doing pretty well in school and could always come home to visit her parents. Maybe Hilary didn't understand.

Her hand had grazed the heel of a pointy stiletto boot when the sound of her cell phone went off. She smiled as her favorite band, Links & Chains, crooned out the chorus to one of their powerhouse songs, Illuminated Lovers. That smile turned into wariness as her eyes took in the display on the screen. An unfamiliar number was calling, which could have been a telemarketer or researcher, but she highly doubted it knowing how quickly Hilary and Tony worked.

"Hello?"

"Hey, this is Lauren, right?"

"Yes," she answered hesitantly.

"Hey, hey, it's Collin."

"Hey, hey, yourself. What's up?"

"Just finished classes for the day. Thinking about setting up a party for tonight."

"Oh?" she questioned.

"Yeah. Wanted to see if you would be around."

It was a question that came across more like a statement. He hardly had to work at getting girls' attention, so maybe that was his usual way of things. She had been to a few of his parties, but they'd barely spoken as far as she could remember.

"Actually, I left early this morning for home and won't be back until Sunday."

"Oh, that's too bad. Tony hadn't mentioned that."

"Sorry," she apologized for no reason.

"Maybe next time then."

"Yeah, you'll have to have double the fun to make up for my

not being there."

The sentence slipped out of her mouth without thinking. What a stupid thing to say.

He chuckled over the line. "I'll see what I can do."

She wasn't sure what to say at this point that wouldn't make her sound like an idiot. Why was she making this a big deal? He was just a guy. She needed to get a grip.

"So what are your plans for the weekend?" Collin asked.

"Laundry and shopping. Nothing too crazy."

"Shopping, huh?" he questioned.

"I'm looking at shoes as we speak," she chuckled nervously.

"I see."

"What's that supposed to mean?"

"Nothing. I've got to head out, but I'll see you around," he said.

"Oh, okay. Bye."

He had already disconnected the call before she even finished saying okay. She was flummoxed at the entire situation. Maybe he wasn't interested in her after all. Hilary's hopefulness had somehow rubbed off on her. Lauren could appreciate good-looking men, and Collin was near the top of that spectrum. She hadn't paid him hardly any attention, though, especially in their night class where she focused her daydreams on Professor Klein. Maybe it was better that way...

Collin ran in different circles than she did. The only reason he even knew her was because of Tony and Taylor. The three of them lived in the same dorm freshman year.

Connecting over sports sealed that relationship. She spent the first two months predominately with Taylor, feeling unsure of campus life. Still, Collin was a near stranger with an attractive, familiar face.

Her phone began singing again in her hand. She waited for the display before answering, and the safety of Taylor's name gave her a reason to breathe easy. It was unusual for him to reach out and call her, which only caused more curiosity.

"What's going on, Taylor?"

"Guess who's coming to The Dome?"

Lauren scrunched her brow in thought. "Music or comedian?"

"Music."

"Jesse Loop?"

"Not even close," he teased. "I thought they were your favorite band."

"Links & Chains!" she shouted over the line. It caused a few heads to turn in her direction with the most obvious stern look coming from her mom. She blushed furiously before taking the call outside on the sidewalk. "Are you serious? When?"

"In a couple of months, actually. Too bad the concert is already sold out," he chuckled.

"You're so incredibly mean!"

"Oh, am I? I guess I'll have to take someone else with the extra ticket I have..."

"Taylor!" she shouted again from shock and excitement.

"I know, I know. I'm awesome."

"You totally are. I just can't believe it. Thank you so much."

"You're welcome. Feel free to do my laundry until then," he said.

"I guess that's an even trade," she admitted, although she couldn't think of a worse option. His laundry was never-ending, and thanks to his active lifestyle, smelled like death times three. Was Links & Chains worth it? Most definitely. She knew she'd have to suck it up.

"What are you doing tonight?" she asked.

"Haven't decided yet. There's a basketball game that a few guys are betting on."

"Don't lose too much," she warned.

"My team isn't playing tonight. It'll be a laugh to watch the struggle between Tony and the guys."

"Well, apparently, there's a party tonight, too. Tony might be distracted by Hilary."

"Who's throwing?" he questioned.

"Collin. He invited me, but obviously I can't go."

"Interesting. That has possibilities."

Lauren rolled her eyes. "Yeah, well, you have fun tonight."

"I always do. See ya."

The rest of the shopping trip, Lauren did her best to try to appease her mom for her outburst at the shoe store. It wasn't that difficult to do, and after a few hours, they were home putting away their bags. Lauren had managed to snag a few long sleeve tops to keep warm as the temperature dipped with the season.

Being surrounded by her roommates had allowed her to open up and really begin to get to know herself. She didn't have to pretend to be what she wasn't in front of them, and neither did they. While Gina had been standoffish about divulging her past relationships, it barely took a few months before Hilary had finagled that information out of her.

Hilary was more or less an open book that Lauren envied. Hilary had nothing to hide and regretted none of her actions. Not that all of them were good, but she always said, 'I can't regret lessons learned from life. That's just stupid.' And while Lauren didn't disagree, she still wasn't willing to broadcast everything. A little mystery was good.

*****

The weekend had sped by in a few short hours, at least that was how she felt as she stared at the clock on the dashboard. It was about eleven in the morning on Sunday. The laundry she carted home seemed to double in amount upon arriving back at campus. Lauren wasted no time griping about it; instead, she grabbed what she could and headed towards the dorm. Luckily, it only took two trips back and forth to get everything inside, leaving Taylor's sheets in the car. She began to open one of her bags of clean laundry, but any interest in putting it all away was diminished by the entrance of her roommates.

Lauren took in Gina's expression and looked to Hilary. "What did you do?"

"Nothing too bad," Hilary chuckled.

"Who are you kidding?" Gina replied. "She signed us up for the talent show."

"Hilary!"

"In my defense—"

"There's no defense. She just wants to try something new," Gina interrupted.

"How did we get tangled into this?" Lauren asked Gina.

"I didn't want to do it alone," Hilary admitted. "Besides, we'd have so much fun doing it together, ya know?"

Lauren had a flurry of responses to give back to her roommate, but the hope in Hilary's eyes stopped her. Hilary was a free spirit, and Lauren knew that, especially after the years together. If only Hilary would realize how much unneeded stress her spirit put on them. The only way to get through this would be to pick an activity that wouldn't be too painful or outlandish to perform.

Gina rolled her eyes, annoyed, but nodded an agreement anyway.

After putting her things away neatly, Lauren's body craved a lie down. She kicked off her shoes and curled up into a ball under her fleece blanket that she kept at the end of the bed for just this reason. It took only two deep cleansing breaths until she was out.

*****

"Lauren!"

Her eyes flew open in a panic as Hilary shook her violently. She searched the room fleetingly as she sat up, but seeing nothing threatening, stared back at her roommate. Hilary's eyes were wide with fear that she couldn't understand.

"What's wrong?" Lauren asked.

"You... I thought you weren't..."

"Me?"

"The cafeteria is going to close soon. I wanted to grab food, and you've been lying there almost all day long," Hilary explained. Lauren glanced at the time on the clock and sure enough, it read half past seven in the evening. "I figured you'd be starving, so I came to check on you, and you weren't... at least it didn't look like you were breathing."

Lauren took in a deep breath but didn't feel any difference with it. Maybe she was just in a deep sleep after the weekend away. What else could it possibly be? She didn't feel as rested as she probably should, but she wasn't as tired as earlier. Lauren shrugged it off and slipped off of the bed.

"I feel fine."

"You were so still, Lauren. It looked like—" Hilary bit her lip, stopping the sentence.

Lauren understood where the conversation was going and wanted to change the direction of it. She had more than enough to worry about. She slid on her shoes and threw on her jacket. "Let's grab food before the cafeteria is closed for the night."

Hilary stayed silent but grabbed her jacket and followed. There was nothing that Lauren could say to placate her roommate into feeling better. She couldn't even make sense of it herself. Had she truly stopped breathing? As they walked out of the dorm and into the night air, she only felt a minor sense of relief that the cafeteria was just a short walk.

The campus was quiet except for the few students walking from building to building. The lampposts lighting the way on the paths toward each destination kept Lauren's eyes flicking from side to side. The cafeteria was going to close its doors in ten minutes; they would be able to get inside in time. They'd have an additional fifteen minutes to quickly consume anything still sitting under the heat lamps.

Finding a table was easy. They dropped their jackets on the backs of two chairs and grabbed trays, looking at the food options. There was always the pizza route, but Lauren wasn't really in the mood. She searched the grill section, but burgers weren't appetizing, either. It seemed this was a wasted trip, at least for her.

Lauren filled up a cup with cranberry juice and sipped it while looking over the salad bar. Hilary had already loaded up her tray with grilled chicken pieces for her salad with extra croutons. Lauren followed her back to the table, trying to think of the edible options she had available back in the room.

"The pickings weren't good tonight. Tomorrow is meatloaf extravaganza night at least," Hilary said.

"I guess popcorn will do. I'm not really hungry anyway."

Hilary picked at her plate for a few seconds with hesitation; it was the only hint Lauren had. Her roommate sighed and looked up with concern. "You didn't hear from Collin, did you?"

"I did, actually."

"Oh? And?" she responded excitedly.

"Hilary, I'm okay. I really don't need to be in a relationship."

"I know that, but you could have fun without being in one, too," she pushed.

"Do I really look that unhappy to you?"

Hilary stopped at that question and put her fork down. "Of course you don't."

"Then why force this on me?"

Hilary shrugged and continued picking at her plate.

It seemed clear that Hilary didn't have an answer to that. Maybe there truly wasn't a reason at all, other than that Hilary cared about her. She could appreciate Hilary's concern, but Lauren would have to think of ways to distract her from her self-appointed quest.

Lauren finished her drink and took it over to the drop off area. A flash of long brown hair walking out of the glass cafeteria doors caught her attention. That's when she recognized the girl as Fallon, going downstairs with her backpack on.

Lauren ran back to the table to retrieve her jacket. "I'll see you back at the room, okay?"

Hilary nodded, finishing up the rest of her dinner.

Lauren donned her jacket, racing out of the cafeteria and down the stairs. She couldn't see Fallon or the direction she went. She knew absolutely nothing about her, other than the fact that Fallon knew something about what happened to her. She just had to.

Fallon probably lived on campus, and the dorms were through the back glass door. She went outside and looked around the grounds, not seeing anyone clearly on the paths. That's when a small object flickered in her line of sight. It was unusual to chase after unknown flickering objects, but what options did she have left? She needed to speak to her.

She hurried after the object in the distance, soon realizing that it was a metal clip dangling from a backpack that caught the light. And as she approached, Lauren realized who the backpack was attached to the closer she got.

What could she say to get Fallon to listen? The last time they spoke, she had all but run away. Now she was stalking her at night like a predator. That thought stopped her on the path in utter bewilderment. *Who thought things like that?* Certainly not a normal person and definitely not her.

Lauren began to turn away in the direction of her dorm just as Fallon stopped walking. Fallon broke out in a sprint towards the side of the Richmond Hall dorm. Before Lauren's mind could catch up with her actions, she, too, ran after her classmate. A single cry reached Lauren's ears that scared her and pushed her even faster.

As she got closer, an older woman grasped the side of the building, trying to stumble up the path. Lauren grabbed her side and helped her over towards a park bench as tremors shook through the woman's body. There was no obvious sign of injury, much to Lauren's relief.

"Are you all right? What happened?" Lauren asked.

"He grabbed me. I think it was a he… I'm almost positive," the woman stated. "I screamed for help, and suddenly I was hitting the ground."

"Stay here," Lauren stated as she ran down the side of the building.

Fallon was nowhere to be seen, but the woman's purse was lying on the ground surrounded by scattered papers. She ran down the back side of the building and noticed two figures tussling in the darkness. It had to be Fallon; no one else had been around. Lauren ran towards them as Fallon became clearer, as well as her martial art moves.

The figure she was fighting was most definitely a guy, easily over six feet in height but not muscular. He was extremely fast, but even still, kept backing away whenever she swung her arm towards him. Lauren couldn't understand it but had to help. She couldn't have these attacks repeated over and over again.

Lauren ran to the side, surprising Fallon who took an elbow to the face from the attacker. Lauren began to take deep breaths and gripped her fists as he stepped up with a cocky smirk. She knew that she wasn't an experienced fighter in any way, but she needed to buy time for Fallon.

He reached for her, and she swung instinctively, only to miss him completely. He swiftly grabbed her, tossing her easily into the building. Lauren didn't get the chance to even catch her breath as he yanked her up from the ground, gripping her by the throat.

She couldn't have screamed even if she wanted to. Her eyes were slightly blurry, but she wasn't going to be a victim. Not again. She used the power in her legs to push off of the building, using the momentum to knee him in the groin. It had less of an effect than she wanted but enough to cause him to let go.

Fallon came up from behind him, but he sidestepped quickly, looking between the two of them. Lauren didn't know what to expect from either of them. He swung at Fallon before dropping down, swiftly taking Lauren's feet out from beneath her. As her head hit the ground, her eyes squeezed shut reflexively from the pain. It had been the second time she'd banged her head in a minute.

He blurred in front of her until she heard the gruff sound of Fallon hitting the ground, too. Then he was on top of Lauren, speaking in tongues she couldn't understand. Her lips formed to speak as he leaned in with clear intent. It was then that Fallon jumped onto his back and his movements stopped completely.

His breath in Lauren's face suddenly disappeared as well as the heaviness of his weight. Right before her eyes, he began to slowly but surely fade away into thin air. Then the weight of Fallon alone was upon her but she couldn't move.

"Why were you following me?" Fallon asked, pressing the tip of a sharp knife to her chest.

"I wasn't—"

Fallon pushed the knife tip farther into her chest. "I'm not an idiot."

"Then stop trying to murder me."

"It wouldn't count as murder," Fallon stated.

"Then you *are* an idiot," Lauren challenged.

Fallon sat up slightly, leaving the knife still against her chest. "We'll see in two nights' time."

Fallon stood, tucked the knife into her jeans, and grabbed her backpack as she walked back towards the path. Lauren's head was throbbing, but she needed to get answers. Panic pushed her forward.

"Wait, please," Lauren begged, getting to her feet. "What happens in two nights?"

Fallon refused to look at her but replied, "The eclipse."

Chapter Four

Lauren had done nothing other than pace the floor of her dorm room almost all night. Her body was full of nervous energy thanks to the traumatic events that led her head to meet against the solid concrete. It was almost fate that after not seeing Fallon for a little more than a week, she just appeared out of nowhere. And if she was concerned enough to help that woman fend off an attacker, why didn't she check on her afterward? She had just walked away.

Fallon had as easily vanished into thin air just like that guy did. Lauren was left to help get the woman's purse and papers back to her. The woman turned out to be a substitute professor, and Lauren fabricated a story about the attacker running away. She certainly couldn't tell *her* the truth. Lauren could only imagine what her reaction would have been. Things were somehow worse now.

What was going to happen to her in two nights' time? If it was because of the attack and whatever it was she had been forced to consume, what could be done to stop it? There was no denying the minor changes within her, like the black veins. She peered down to her hands, taking the in the vivid exterior. Fallon had the information Lauren needed, though, but could she find her again?

Who could she even talk to about this? Taylor was an option, but she had been feeling so strange the last time she was near him. He wasn't having any of the issues she was—or at least he wasn't mentioning anything. The last time she'd seen him, his veins were normal and only had the strange fading effect on his shoulder.

Her energy levels were increasing, although when she slept, it was hard enough to scare her roommates into thinking she'd stopped breathing. She could still see the fear in Hilary's eyes. The chest-rumbling incident hadn't happened again. While she had feared walking the campus at night, that seemed to have dissipated. Apparently, she was the thing to be feared, as Fallon would tell it.

Fallon had said that she'd turn into one of them—the attacker from that night and tonight; she had to find a way to keep that from happening. What could she do to stop it?

Lauren searched the web for anything that fell into place about her attack. The only things that even slightly resembled her circumstances were folklore and movies, which of course weren't factual. Fallon stated an eclipse was involved, so werewolves baying at the full moon were more than ruled out. Vampires came close, too, being ruled by the night, but they had to be staked by wood. The detail that she wasn't bitten and the weird fading aspect ruled vampires out even further. Everyone knew that vampires poofed into dust.

She went to the full-length mirror, tugging her hair back to examine her neck. There was barely a bruise to see. Without thinking, she opened her mouth, examining her gum line and teeth for any changes. When her eyes met with her own in the mirror, she laughed without humor. The small, red veins in her eyes that used to stand out against the white had turned black, too. This was the most ridiculous thing she'd ever seen.

The sun was beginning to rise only to confirm her suspicions of time moving way too quickly. Since sleep wasn't going to come after all, she showered for the day, spending the few hours reading ahead in her classes for preparation. Maybe she would be able to search through the library for more information after classes. There had to be something; the attacks couldn't be as rare as they seemed.

*****

Lauren arrived back to the dorm room ready to kick off her shoes and pass out when she realized that Tony and Hilary were talking. When they looked up and smiled awkwardly, it made her want to run in the opposite direction. It wasn't a happy-to-see you smile. It was a we've-caught-you-now smile that set off the alarms.

She thumbed back towards the hall. "Bad time?"
Hilary shook her head. "No, just waiting for Collin."
Lauren glared at her roommate knowingly.
Tony laughed before turning it into a cough. "We're working on a project, Lauren."

She ignored both of them, struggling to keep upright as exhaustion pressured her body. She had a sinking feeling that if she stayed, Hilary would be up to her matchmaking tricks. Lauren checked the time on her cell phone and knew Taylor didn't have class for an hour. She sent him a quick text asking if she could stop over with the laundered sheets. It would be a sneak attack he wouldn't see coming.

He responded as she expected with acceptance, and she gathered his duffle containing the sheets while heading for the door. Hilary glanced up as the door opened, but Lauren didn't give her a chance to inquire before rushing out of it. Her physical and mental states were in question already; the last thing she needed to add was a guy.

In no time at all, she was at the door waiting for Taylor to let her into the building. When he appeared on the other side of the door, she questioned herself again on why he seemed so normal after everything when she wasn't.

"Hey, Lauren, thanks for this," he said. Noticing she wasn't leaving, he added, "You wanna come up?"

"Door to door service and all that."

Taylor only laughed, holding the door open for her to walk through. He took the duffle bag from her before they began to ascend the stairs. She wasn't even out of breath by the time they reached his room. Taylor was more conditioned for the walk up, but even he seemed more than a bit energized by it.

"So, how excited are you?" Taylor asked as they went into the room.

"Very?" she asked, unsure of the question.

"Links—"

She could feel her cheeks lift and blush at the same time. "You have no idea. Hunter has the most amazing voice I've ever heard!"

"Whatever. The band has good music."

"Why did you offer me a ticket? I mean, I'm very grateful, but any girl you asked would be," Lauren said, settling into the desk chair.

"If you don't want to go—"

"I do!" Lauren exclaimed loudly. "I was just curious."

Taylor smirked as he started shoving some notebooks into his backpack. "You're not a pain in the ass. I can enjoy the show without having to get things for you."

She couldn't find the words to respond. He had complimented her more in the last two weeks than the last three years. Not that she had been looking for that; it was just very unexpected. She accepted his explanation and began to pull the sheets from the duffle bag. They still smelled like the dryer sheet from home.

"Do you want me to put these on the other bed?"

Taylor shook his head. "I'll strip my bed when I get back."

Lauren still hadn't broached the reason for her visit and knew it had to be now. She wasn't going to touch his current sheets if she could help it. She was more than aware that sleep wasn't the only thing that took place within them. Relationships weren't sealed in bedroom activities. Time had slipped away; it was now or never.

"Would you mind if I crashed here for a bit?"

"Sure," he replied, but after a minute followed up with, "Why?"

"Too much traffic in my room, and I'm so tired. I just need peace and quiet."

He didn't say anything, almost like he was pressing her for further explanation without asking. She stared at her shoes, hoping that the silence would placate him into just stripping the bed. It was surprising when he sat down on the edge of the bed facing her.

"Is this about what happened? The attack?"

Lauren shook her head. "I just need space, but Hilary is so..."

"Are you sure?"

"Forget it. I'll just go," she said, heading for the door.

Taylor grabbed her arm, tugging her back to face him. "Don't pull that shit on me. If you're afraid, just say it."

"Hil—"

"Lauren," he warned.

She glared at him as her composure finally began to run out. "Hilary is trying to set me up with Collin. I'm not ready to… I just don't want to deal with it. She had invited him over to talk to Tony, but I know that wasn't the only reason why."

Taylor's face remained composed, waiting for her to admit something more. She couldn't understand how he knew when she was holding back information from him. It wasn't like she had even meant to keep it a secret; it just wasn't on her mind to bring it up.

"And… I was walking back from the cafeteria last night and someone was attacked. We ran to help her. She escaped unscathed, fortunately, but we couldn't say the same for the attacker."

His expression became severe; his eyes were as dark as coffee and staring daggers at her. "We?"

"This girl from class, Fallon, and I—"

"How are you just telling me this now? Did you go to the cops?" he interrupted.

"I was having trouble getting my thoughts together after being thrown against the building," Lauren stated, trying to escape his grasp. "We don't have to worry about him anymore, though."

"And why is that?"

"He's dead," Lauren said matter-of-factly.

Taylor sucked in a large breath, unsure of how to respond. It was obvious that he thought she was insane, but the fact that he had been attacked with her seemed to keep him on her side. At least as much as he could mentally accept all at once. There had to be a better way of explaining this, but she had failed to find one. In his shocked stance, she removed her arm from his grasp and sat back down at the desk, not looking at him. He kept staring at her from the door as she described the details.

"And he just faded away?" he asked in disbelief when she finished.

Lauren nodded, keeping silent to allow the information to sink in fully. He hadn't moved an inch towards the door, which was a good sign. She decided to ground the end of the story with something he could really see with his own eyes. She stood before him, tugging the sleeves of her hoodie up her arms.

"If you can believe this," she said, showing off the dark veins of her hands, "then you can believe what I'm telling you. There's something majorly wrong going on out there at night. It's not safe."

Taylor couldn't refute that, but he swallowed hard before asking,

"Two nights from now?"

"I'm going to research later," she said.

"Not without me, you aren't."

The trip to the library was filled with tension and unasked questions between them. After searching for the mythical and folklore sections, they realized it was all kept down in the basement level. As she went down the stairs, the smell of muskiness welcomed her. At this point, she was ready to consider Zombies real, and this was just a step to the beginning of the apocalypse.

They grabbed a few books, skimming through the pages for some clarification. She was going for her fourth round of shelf picking when Taylor called her back to the table. When she reached his side, his expression was crossed between irritated and astonished. He didn't even wait for her to take a seat, pointing to a middle paragraph on the page.

"Feeds primarily at night on beautiful, unsuspecting women," he laughed humorlessly. "Leaving a strange black substance to spread throughout her system."

Lauren's eyes flew open. "Does it say how long it lasts for?"

"It doesn't, which leads me to believe that it won't ever change. I'm sorry." Taylor glanced back at the book. "The victim's memory of the encounter will vanish."

"I haven't forgotten. I remember what happened."

"What did the attacker look like?" he asked.

She opened her mouth to respond and faltered. Everything had happened so fast, she didn't get a good look. But shouldn't she remember something? When her eyes met Taylor's, they matched in somberness.

"It faced me. It attacked me face to face, and I can't describe it at all. Not even eye color, not hair color… it was tall, but that's it. Does it say anything about the eclipse?" she asked.

He sat back in his chair with a grunt. "No."

Lauren picked through the books she had brought back to the table. The information was either too unreal or not close enough to be the same. She wondered how she could trust a book about what she had been through when she knew the person with the answer was on campus. They were running out of time.

"What's that?" he asked, pointing to the picture in front of her.

It was a depiction of a wolf howling at the moon. The description below only stated the same. The moon was partially hidden by a cloud with no further anomaly. Lauren wasn't exactly sure what she was looking for, but werewolf had been crossed off of the list right away. It certainly wasn't an overgrown mutt that attacked them.

Taylor pulled the book in front of him reading the paragraphs beside the picture. He read a couple of pages until he flipped back and forth between the two books. Taylor pointed to the passage he read about memory loss after the attack and back to the passage by the moon.

"They're connected. Not like one plus one equals two, but on the same page. It's like the books were ripped apart with pages separated," he said.

When she looked deeper at the books, it became clearer. The pages were slightly off color from the rest of the book. The font was close but not perfectly the same as the books they were clearly from. Her eyes lit with a mission. She skimmed through the rest of the book with the moon picture, but determined only three pages were added.

Taylor skimmed his book, too, and only three pages were included as well. There was a pattern. On a mission, they both went through all the books looking for the three pages that didn't exactly match and made copies to go over back at the dorm. There were nine books in total that they found and scanned.

"Do you think there's more?"

Lauren glanced at her cell phone. "I'm not sure, but we're out of time."

"Let's take these back to my room," he suggested.

"Okay, but I can't stay too late."

Taylor shrugged, collecting the papers they had scanned, while she took the few to the counter she hadn't had time to go through. If there was something hiding somewhere, there wasn't a lot of time to research. The eclipse was only one night away. Lauren cringed at the thought while the girl behind the desk scanned her books and college ID.

Lauren met Taylor at the exit to the library and they made their way across campus to his dorm room. He pulled out the scanned papers to begin reading while she began to flip through the pages of the first book.

"Every attack is different, and the victims' body reactions vary. It is a telltale sign of what the future holds. The attack is merely that; however, should the gene run through the victim's body, it will make the change more likely," he read.

"Then what does that have to do with the eclipse?"

He shook his head. "That isn't mentioned on this page. Maybe it's on another?"

Lauren finished scanning through the first book, finding nothing inside. She picked up the next in hopes of finding something about the eclipse. That's when she came across a diagram that she recognized from biology. It was a simple picture of a chromosome but shattered into pieces with description of how it made up a person. And then she realized how it could be taken apart under scientific scrutiny.

Lauren buried herself in the research along with Taylor until she could barely keep her eyes open. When she did manage to reopen them again, she was surprised by the stiffness in her neck. It was then that she realized the time and began to panic. She had missed her first class of the day and was soon to be late to the next one. She swore under her breath as she collected her things, giving Taylor a shove as she passed by the bed. He was surrounded by their research papers, fast asleep.

"Wake up!" she said, shoving him again. "We're gonna miss another class."

He mumbled a bit until she shoved him one last time. "I have to go. Get up."

"I'm up," he said, even though he hadn't opened his eyes. "I'm up."

"Tonight, I have night class with Fallon. Maybe she'll show, but I have to get back on schedule. Don't go back to sleep," Lauren warned.

"I'm up," he repeated, although he hadn't moved an inch.

"We've only got one night left. Let's make the most of the time we have," she said before exiting his room.

Chapter Five

She couldn't help thinking that everything would turn out okay. It just had to, didn't it? There was no way that she could handle being a creature that attacked people. She wasn't an overly emotional person and could withstand certain amounts of pain if she needed to, but this was different. She would be causing harm to others.

Her classes weren't filled with homework since tests were scheduled for the end of the week. The only problem was that it left enough room in her mind to wonder about the unknown. The little information she'd read only barely touched on the really important parts.

Lauren had no appetite at all. Her stomach churned for sustenance, but she just couldn't bring herself to consume anything. Instead, she grabbed a pomegranate drink to placate her basic needs while her mind continued to spiral around her. The chair barely grazed her recognition as she sat down in her historic theatre course.

"You always get here early?"

She knew that voice clearly, although she wish she didn't. "If you're on time, you're late. If you're early, you're on time."

"Where'd you hear that?" Collin asked, taking a seat beside her.

"Band teacher back in high school."

"What'd you play?"

"Flute," she replied.

"You still play?"

"Not so much anymore. Mostly when I'm home on break. Do you play?"

"Not my type of thing," he responded. "It'd be cool to hear you play, though."

Lauren could feel her heart rate start to pick up with adrenaline. She refused to say anything to that. She didn't have time for a guy. Maybe if she kept repeating that to herself, it would feel true.

"Are you ready for the midterm?" she asked.

"Yeah, this one is easy."

Lauren nodded, taking the time to acknowledge Professor Klein along with a few students who'd arrived. Fallon hadn't been one of them, and Lauren wasn't quite sure that she would show up. She could only hope that the upcoming midterm meant something to her.

That small amount of hope began to wither away as class began and there was still no sign of Fallon. Professor Klein practically floated around the room with an air of certainty that the entire class would pass. Whether that optimism was from his teaching or the course material wasn't clear. He prattled on for almost an hour before calling an early dismissal. He wanted us to have more time to study if needed.

Lauren could feel the air whoosh right out of her lungs. If class ended early, then she definitely wouldn't see Fallon. What could she do? Who else was there that she could turn to for information? She gathered her belongings together, not even noticing that Collin had continued a discussion with her.

When they walked outside of the building, she caught sight of a figure that resembled Fallon. The girl was talking with a guy but kept looking over her shoulder in a curious manner. Lauren hadn't realized her feet had headed in that direction until Collin's voice broke through.

"So you'll be there?"

"Be where?" she asked, confused.

Collin looked at her quizzically. "Saturday night. The kegger?"

Lauren nodded quickly. "Yeah, of course."

She had no clue about what he was going on about, but she had to get to Fallon. She could see he was clearly going to keep talking, and she didn't have a moment to spare.

"I have to run. I'll see you Thursday," she said, not waiting for a reply.

With every step, she was surer that she had the right person. It was strange seeing Fallon react to another person without fear or anger. She seemed to stick close, even holding the boy's hand, until she looked up and kissed him. Lauren felt guilty breaking into their moment, but her life was at stake. There would be time for rekindling later.

"Fallon..."

The words merely left her lips on a loud whisper as she recognized someone else. Fallon's eyes flicked in Lauren's direction along with a pair of vibrant blue that she'd never be able to mistake. His eyes began to squint into what she remembered as a guilty reaction as his cheeks flushed, and not only from the cold. When Lauren had a moment to even take in Fallon's expression again, it had changed from annoyed to confused.

"Lauren," Quinn began. "Hey."

"What do you want?" Fallon asked, falling back into irritability.

"I-I researched but—"

Fallon laughed without humor. "There's no cure."

"Wait. Lauren was the girl?" Quinn asked.

"It's not a problem. Until she becomes a problem," Fallon stated.

Lauren snapped her attention to Fallon. "Why won't you help me?"

"There's nothing I can do. There's nothing anyone can do," Fallon admitted seriously. "Only the sun can save you now."

"*What does that mean?*"

Quinn sighed, frustrated, but it appeared to be aimed more at Fallon than herself. "When the eclipse happens, it breaks apart the chromosomes in your DNA thanks to the virus that's been introduced from the attack. It's rare, but some people don't change. It's something to do with their DNA," he explained.

"Very rarely does that happen, but sometimes, the sun keeps those who have been infected grounded, evaporating the virus within them," she finished.

"I'd still be me," Lauren confirmed.

"Mostly. Some things won't be the same anymore, but yeah," Quinn said.

Lauren was at a loss for words. There was only a small chance that she wouldn't turn into some pillaging beast, infecting people left and right, inflicting mayhem on the innocent, which seemed to cast a shadow over her mind. She had so many questions about what her future would be. If she would have to leave the state, what would she eat, what explanation would she give her parents? But as she stood there with Quinn looking at her intently, she wanted nothing more than to scream.

She was going to turn into a monster. Something that could hurt people and change who she was. She'd be the nightmare of every child's dream, except she would be real.

Lauren sucked in a deep, cold breath as she felt tears prick at her eyes. She ran down the path away from both of them. She had no sense of direction, but when her fingers gripped the car handle, it felt right. She slid into the vehicle and took off towards the highway.

Although the CD playing Links & Chains blared at top volume, nothing was penetrating her senses. The highway was oddly clear for a weeknight. Exits blurred past in the darkness. The sound of ringing caught her attention only as the music came to a stop. The phone number lit up over the dashboard only making the urge to sob aloud stronger. She knew she had to answer the call, but everything inside wanted her to push the gas pedal harder.

"Hello?"

"Where are you?" Taylor inquired.

"Why?"

"I'm standing at your door and no one is answering," he replied. "So?"

"We're in trouble."

"What kind of trouble?" he asked.

Lauren sniffed and wiped her cheek with one hand, trying to think where to start. There were details that he needed to know, but she was so afraid she could barely think. How could she tell her best friend that they were going to turn into monsters? It wasn't that the possibility wasn't there before, but the chances of it becoming true were set in reality now. There was no mistaking it.

"Are you crying?"

"Shut up, Taylor," she demanded.

"You are, aren't you? Where are you?"

"I don't know," she moaned, sniffing again. "I'm going south on the highway."

"Lauren, turn around."

"I don't want to," she admitted.

"Come back and pick me up. We can go anywhere tonight."

The last thing she wanted to do was turn back towards campus. She didn't want to be near anyone, although Taylor was the exception. He was in the same situation as she was. At least she wouldn't be putting him in danger. Not really. She swiped her face again, agreeing to pick him up in the parking lot.

It took almost twenty minutes to get back to get him, but she didn't waste time. He buckled up, and she took off. She started to head south with no destination in mind. Something inside encouraged this option, and she couldn't process anything beyond that. She couldn't even bring herself to look at Taylor now that he was sitting beside her.

Taylor turned the volume of the music down allowing the silence to take over the car. He patiently waited for her to explain. She could barely speak over a whisper, but he heard her just the same.

"There's no cure," he repeated.

She could only shake her head. He sighed loudly but didn't say anything, either. Whatever he was thinking, he didn't feel like sharing, not that she could blame him. They continued for another hour until the gas light came on.

Lauren pulled into the next gas station, slipping out of the car as soon as she put it in park. She went to the gas pump, slid her card through for payment and began to fill the tank. She stared at the empty road contemplating where they would end up tonight. Was it beyond crazy that as much as she felt the need to get away from campus, she was worried about exams?

When she climbed back into the vehicle, the urge to continue going south had subsided. There was nothing other than the sounds of their breathing echoing inside the car. Lauren started the car, turning it back towards the campus with few options left.

"Why did you come by my room, anyway?" she asked finally.

"Dad called to say that Marcus was getting into trouble back home," he admitted, staring out the window. "He thinks he should come up here to get a break from his friends."

Lauren was well aware of the trouble Marcus had caused most of Taylor's childhood. She had to watch Taylor clean up his younger brother's messes more than a few times. Even she covered for him every once in a while, but he never seemed to stay out of trouble. Taylor was dealing with the same devastating family situation as Marcus, but Marcus selfishly lashed out in response. It was only getting worse with Taylor away at college and soon to be graduating.

"Did he say when?" she asked.

"No, but he can't come now…"

She understood why he couldn't come with their humanity now in question. For a moment, she began to imagine what it would be like to have Marcus see them both as monsters. Would it be enough to scare him straight? Probably not. He'd want to join in the massacre.

The time on the dashboard read half past two in the morning as she pulled into the parking lot. As they climbed out of the vehicle and walked across the campus, it was eerily silent. Not even a breeze brushed their skin, like even Mother Nature knew not to get too close. She shook off the dark thought as they approached his dorm. She didn't need to ask, and he didn't say anything as they went inside for the night.

Chapter Six

Lauren felt like a tuning fork all morning long. Everything was out of focus and lingered longer than it was supposed to. Passing the midterm was hardly the concern it had been. Instead, every hiccup, every cough or sneeze was setting her internal alarm to possible changes within her.

When she finished her last midterm for the day, it was only two in the afternoon. Too much time to worry and not enough to get the space that she needed. As she trudged back to her dorm, it seemed the distance had stretched. She knew her perception was untrustworthy and chose to sit down on a bench.

Lauren looked up to the sky and said a silent prayer. Maybe there was a greater chance of not turning than people believed? Maybe if she prayed hard enough, she and Taylor would be saved. With the sun warming her cheeks, she thought of all the struggles they'd been through together. Certainly, people couldn't always have bad things happening to them, or they'd never realize it was bad. The good had to balance it out at some point, didn't it?

The pressure of the bench lessened beneath her, a subtle notification of company. She kept her eyes closed, focusing on keeping calm. Never once had she tried to fool herself into thinking the change wasn't possible; there was too much evidence that it was.

"Do you have plans for tonight?"

"Apparently, I do," Lauren replied, glancing at Quinn.

He ignored her response. "Will you come with me?"

"What for?"

"Were you planning to go through this with Gina and Hilary

watching?"

"Why should I trust you? Won't you and Fallon be waiting to stab me at the first chance you get?" she asked, staring across the campus lawn.

It had been more than an eye opening experience watching Fallon take on the last attacker. She was skilled and ready, and this time, she knew who would be changing. Lauren couldn't deny the nightmares she had where she took the place of the attacker and Fallon easily slid in the knife. No, she did not want to be a monster, but she certainly wasn't in a mindset to be killed, either.

"She wouldn't..." Noticing Lauren's raised eyebrows, he began again, "I wouldn't let her hurt you. Not if by some miracle you didn't turn tonight."

There were too many layers that she wasn't willing to touch in that response. Besides, she couldn't just leave Taylor. And worse, she wouldn't want to give them that information if they were going to hurt them both. She couldn't hand over her best friend like that, monster or not.

"I'll keep that in mind."

"Lauren, you have no idea what it's going to be like. Turning into a Sanguis Bellator is no joke."

That broke through the barrier. "Sang-what?"

"It's Latin for Blood Warrior. There's so much you don't even know. Let me help you," he pled.

Her insides clenched at the idea of allowing him to help, but she couldn't decide if it was fear of what he'd tell her or the pain of being dumped by him. Could she risk ignoring information that might help her because of their past? That left only one option.

"How can you help? You said there is no cure."

Quinn stood up. "There isn't. But there are ways of making the transition easier."

*****

"Watch your head," he said, ducking under a fallen beam.

"What is this place?" she asked, trying not to touch anything.

"A forgotten treasure."

Lauren glanced around, noticing the peeling paint on the walls and even more beams hanging from the ceiling. Cobwebs dangled and dust floated through the air as they walked. She took careful steps hearing the floor creak beneath their feet. When he approached the staircase to the basement, she gave him a dubious look.

"We've reinforced the stairs, but be careful," he stated.

"Is it too late to change my mind...?" she muttered.

"You've come this far. Don't be a spoil sport now."

Lauren grit her teeth but said nothing. He waited for her to reach the bottom before continuing into the next room. It was less shabby than the upstairs but only in that most of the deterioration had been collectively pushed into one corner. There were two black desks covered in test tubes, beakers and an old school Bunsen burner.

"You made a lab?"

"Salvaged. This used to be the science building until one freak accident. The administration decided it was better to build a better one and tear this one down," Quinn stared at the room with a smile. "Isn't

74

she beautiful?"

Lauren had nothing nice to say and chose to tread lightly. "I don't have much time left..."

He seemed to sober up instantly and encouraged her to follow him towards one of the cabinets lined against the wall. He combed through a few vials before handing her two. One was the color of the Mediterranean Sea, luminously green. The other was unmistakable—blood.

She looked into his eyes, full of questions she didn't want to ask but knew she needed the answers to. He didn't wait for her to ask, gesturing with his hand for to take a seat on a nearby stool. He stood behind the desk fiddling with the Bunsen burner.

"The sun will set about a quarter 'til seven. The eclipse usually takes place around two in the morning," he explained, filling a beaker with water. "I can't tell you what it's going to feel like, but I can tell you what I've seen."

Dread filled her as he grabbed a small vial of burnt orange-colored liquid. "The human body is mainly composed of water. After you were infected, a virus was introduced." He used a dropper, allowing two drops of the liquid to fall into the beaker. The color tinted the water, but it wasn't a drastic change. He used a stirrer to swirl the water and still it was only muted.

"I can see the hope in your eyes, and I don't wish to discourage it. You need to be prepared..." Quinn placed the beaker onto the Bunsen burner and watched as it slowly heated. "The human body temperature is only ninety-eight point five on a normal day. We know we have a fever if it hits one hundred or higher. Your body will break into feverish sweats that no amount of water can quench."

The water began to boil causing massive amounts of steam to jolt from the top, slowly eating away at the vast amount of water. It was silent as the level went down until there was nothing left other than the yellowish liquid stuck to the bottom. Suddenly, that began to dry up and burn before her eyes causing a different kind of smoke.

"Eventually the heat will sizzle out." He turned off the burner placing a small fan beside it. "When you finally cool down, there will be nothing left but the virus in whatever state it leaves you in after the change."

Her eyes widened. "You make it sound like I'm going to d..."

Quinn nodded slowly. "There's a possibility that you might not make it." He placed his hand over hers gently. "Please stay here. We can help you after the outcome, but if you're alone, who will find you? Who would know where you were or what they'd find—"

She slid off of the stool in revulsion before she realized she'd made that decision. She couldn't process what he was saying. No, that wasn't it. She didn't want to process it. She didn't want any of this, and before she knew it, she was at the top of the stairs.

Frozen in shock, she stared around her surroundings taking in the dust motes floating around. There was no real explanation of how she came to be upstairs, and the more she tried to think it through, the more her head began to ache with slowness. The creak of the floorboards behind her only seemed to agitate her as she whirled on him.

"You're fast. Not everyone is lucky enough to get that side effect."

76

"I didn't—"

"Mean to? It's part of the virus. The person who infected you had that ability. You will have some of the same traits, but some will be unique only to you," he said.

"How do you know all of this? Why am I supposed to believe you?"

"You're not the first Bellator I've met, and you won't be the last. Unfortunately, this seems to be part of my family history," he admitted.

Another creak in the floorboards sent their attention towards the door. Lauren knew exactly who it would be. It wasn't like this building was a well-known or used facility. It only took a few steps before Fallon's figure came into view with her hair piled in a high ponytail.

"Unbelievable. You got her to come?"

Quinn made his way between them. "It wasn't that hard."

Dread started coursing through Lauren. Was this a set up? Were they just going to trap her here anyway? She had already seen Fallon's fighting skills, and even with her speed, Lauren couldn't outrun both of them. Quinn would find a way to stop her.

"I have to go..."

"Lauren, we've discussed this," he said.

"I have more than enough time to come back. The eclipse is hours away."

Fallon glared at him. "The eclipse doesn't begin the change. It ends it."

"But you said... What about the sun?" Lauren fumbled for anything. As panic began to sink in that they weren't going to allow her to leave, her time was truly coming to a close.

"When the sun sets, it begins. But from what I can see, you're already making adjustments," Quinn stated.

"There's nowhere for you to run, Lauren. No safe place for you out there. No safe place for the innocents if you're out there," Fallon said.

Fallon was looking at her in a strange way. She wasn't friendly in the least, but she did care about keeping the peace. Why, of all things, would she care? Lauren wanted nothing more than to get back in her car and drive away like she had before, but Fallon was right. She'd be putting people in danger.

That's when her mind clicked and honed onto one thought: Taylor. He had no clue about what would happen to him; and worse, he'd be surrounded by people. What other options did they have?

"I'm not staying here because I don't trust either one of you. You'd kill me on sight, no questions asked. I'm not a complete idiot. But I don't want to hurt anyone. Where would be the next safest place?" Lauren asked with determination, making her back stiff.

"Lauren—"

"You've informed me, and I'm... appreciative. I still have a choice, though, and the mere fact that there is a minor chance that I might not turn..." Fallon gave her a look of complete idiocy. "I have a right to do this alone."

She made a point to start making her way out of the room slowly as to not scare them and give them time to answer her. It wasn't until she reached the doorway that Quinn spoke up.

"Isolation is the only guarantee. The offer still stands if you change your mind."

Lauren thanked them with a curt nod and took off towards her dorm. Time was of the essence, after all. She was relieved to find the room empty as she grabbed a handful of clothes and her phone charger. She slipped her car keys into her jacket pocket and made a quick trip to her car.

She dialed Taylor, but his phone rang into voicemail. Maybe he had an exam? She couldn't be sure. Her fingers gripped the car keys feeling the same intense urge to get in the car and drive. There was no way she could leave him behind, not with all she knew. He deserved better than that.

Lauren ducked into the first academic building she could see. The call of nature was still giving its natural alert and she paid close attention. Going into the first stall, she used the facility and went to wash her hands. She couldn't bring herself to even look in the mirror. There was nothing she wanted to reflect on.

When she made her way out of the building, Collin came into view. He was leaving the same building from another door, completely oblivious to her presence. Her thoughts hadn't caught up to her actions when she found herself in step with him. His eyes lifted significantly at her arrival, which conflicted with his too-cool-to-care attitude.

"You done for the day?"

She could only nod, wanting to ignore the double meaning she heard. "You?"

"I have one more, but it'll be quick," he said. "Where you headed?"

She suddenly stepped in front of him, not wanting to walk farther. "Umm… not this way. I just wanted to say hi."

He smirked cockily. "That's all?"

"Yeah." Lauren couldn't bring herself to say any more. It was as if her brain and mouth were getting disconnected. She couldn't even remember why she had approached him in the first place. She already knew he was unattainable; maybe the current situation was only forcing her to truly acknowledge the truth.

Collin chuckled. "All right. Well, I guess I'll see you tomorrow at the exam."

"Yeah, see you then..." she said, disheartened.

He walked away, and she found herself wishing for things to go back to normal. It was only worse that the change hadn't even begun yet. Maybe she could have proven herself to be worthy of his attention. She wouldn't be worthy of anything after tonight.

"Lauren?" She turned to find Taylor with a puzzled expression. "Trying to make it work?"

"Huh?"

"With Collin," he pushed.

She shook her head. "I'm not... no."

He took in her hesitant response. "What's wrong?"

"Are you done with exams?"

"Yeah. Why?" he asked.

"We need to go somewhere to be alone. Grab some clothes and meet me in the car."

"Now?"

She could only nod, as she headed back to the vehicle. Explaining everything to Taylor scared her. It was one thing to hear it herself, but repeating it somehow made it more real.

Chapter Seven

Lauren stepped out of the car after a long drive, unsure of the next move. She knew that Taylor had a lot to think about with minimal time. What else could she offer him?

Lauren could only hope that this was all a nightmare and she would wake up. She wasn't sure what to expect, but from the details that Quinn explained, she had picked up some extra items she might need. Taylor was quiet, but she could see the horror in his eyes when he looked at her. She made a point to not look at him any longer.

Somehow, she had caused this to affect him, too. She was attacked and because he cared enough to fight for her, he was bitten. He was part of this mess because of her. Guilt lanced her swiftly as though she were a marshmallow. There had to be more to offer him than this. There had to be more for herself than waiting the last half-hour for the sun to set. At least she knew no one would find them here at his uncle's cabin, and there weren't a great deal of people in the area.

Her mouth was dry, and she sipped her water bottle to moisten it. Maybe that was a symptom? Was it starting already? Quinn mentioned that she was already adjusting. She forced herself to take slow, deep breaths. Freaking out wasn't going to help anyone.

Taylor brought in the last of the blankets and began to assemble them on the floor of the living room after pushing the couch against the wall. Every move he made was methodical, and after fixing up their resting area, he began to pull out the chairs and candles.

The cooler was brought closer to their bedding area, along with a big bowl and washcloths. Taylor took his time filling the bowl with ice cubes as Lauren paced around the room. She checked her phone only to pace with more intensity. There was about fifteen minutes before sunset, and all she could do was think of what she hadn't accomplished in time. She'd already caught herself multiple times wanting to voice aloud her complaints to Taylor.

"Hungry?" Taylor asked, grabbing a bag of chips from his backpack.

Lauren wanted to vomit at the sight of the bag. "Ew."

"Come on, they have ridges..."

"How can you possibly eat?" she questioned.

"Easy," he said, shoving a handful of chips in his mouth. "This is a shitty situation. The least we can do is enjoy junk on the way."

Her stomach started churning as he crunched on the offending snack. "No, thanks."

"What will your favorite food memory be? Something recent," he pushed.

"I don't have one."

"Not at all? You like meatloaf night at the cafeteria."

She shook her head. "I haven't been... participating for a while."

Taylor stopped chewing to gawk. "Starving yourself? What? A new diet?"

"No... I'm just not hungry."

"Ever?"

Lauren shook her head noting that he clearly didn't feel the same. Pacing was all that she could think about. Moving felt right; maybe she could move fast enough to avoid it. She did about three circuits before Taylor stepped in her way.

"Your blurring is making me nauseous."

"How can you be so calm?!" Lauren finally exclaimed. "I want to claw out of my own skin!"

His eyes seemed to darken with her words. "One, you're sweating. Two, I'm not calm, but I don't wear my feelings on my forehead. Three, would freaking out change the outcome?"

"Stop being so mentally controlling!" she yelled as she began to pace around him. "Maybe this was a bad idea… maybe I should go back—"

"To Quinn?" he asked disgustedly.

"Taylor, there was limited information in those books we found. We don't even know what will happen to us."

"You thought they were going to kill you. What made you change your mind now?" he asked.

She stopped walking and took a deep breath. He was speaking the truth, and she couldn't deny that. She hadn't trusted them; still, her fear was high enough that that minor detail was slowly starting to lose its importance. She didn't want to be alone, not like this.

The sweat was dripping from her scalp down her forehead and down the back of her neck. When did it become so hot? She knew the answer right away and made herself busy, grabbing ice cubes to shove into her mouth. Taylor sat across from her on his self-made bedding, silently watching her actions.

Time was ticking away, and not watching it was like not watching the countdown on a microwave. Her eyes flicked to her phone multiple times before she dunked the washcloth into the bowl with melted ice cubes and put it over her eyes, lying down. She could feel her heart pounding away in her chest as her body began to break out into a cold sweat. Even her toes were sweating.

With her eyes squeezed shut tightly, she forced thoughts of a paradise vacation. She would be lounging on a powder soft beach with her toes in the sand. Her sunglasses blocking out the sun wouldn't taint the beauty of the aquatic ripples that splashed at the shore. The fruity umbrella drink, still cool in her hand, would cause her taste buds to beg for more. And she would give in to it; there was nowhere else she had to be.

"What would you like to do?"

Lauren looked over to find Quinn lying on the lounge beside her. His hair was playfully mussed up under the summer sun, and he held a beer in his grip. His eyes were covered in dark sunglasses as he leaned up on his elbow. She sighed softly, trying to ignore his attempt to ruin her enjoyable moment.

"I'd like to stay. It's so lovely here."

"For now, but you know it won't stay this way," he advised.

"Why can't it? Everything is harsh and rough elsewhere."

Her back ached as she rolled onto it. The heat was intensifying, and as she looked around, she couldn't find her bag of suntan lotion. There was nothing other than their drinks and the lounge chairs. As she looked around them, the beach was isolated, leaving her feeling even more at home.

"It's not an easy decision, but the important ones never are."

Lauren frowned in his direction. "I have time."

"You'll only cause yourself more pain waiting..." Quinn stated, pointing at her exposed skin that was turning a bright red color.

Her skin felt as if it had ignited with his words. She was

uncomfortably warm, but there was no shelter to hide under, only the small beach blanket she lay on, but that couldn't stop this. She questioned him with her eyes in a panic, but he wouldn't react. He wouldn't offer to help at all.

"Maybe it's time for a swim..."

She stood up feeling the weakness in her legs. Her steps were unsteady as she began, but the heat of the sand had her soon running towards the water. Sprinting into the water was her only thought until she was deep enough to dunk beneath. As she sank below, a scream broke through, sending bubbles to the surface. She swam as hard as she could to the surface and screeched trying to get back to the shore. The water was boiling her alive.

When she finally managed to get back to the shore, the sand was mercilessly sizzling. In what kind of hell had she found herself? Her lounge chair was gone, along with Quinn. She was completely alone. Lauren couldn't get back in the water, and the sand offered no help.

She began running down the shoreline. There had to be someone, somewhere, something to help her. She ran until her legs could barely keep her standing, her feet blistered on the underside and her shoulders were peeling so severely that she couldn't even raise her arms for help without fear that her skin would fall off the bones.

Exhausted, she crumbled to the ground, feeling the sting of the sand pierce her back and legs. The tears she wanted to cry dried up in her tear ducts. She was going to die all alone.

"Please... don't leave me. I don't want to be all alone," her blistered lips pled to the sky.

A shadow covered her face for a moment of relief from the

brutality of the sun. "What do you choose?"

Quinn stood before her holding the vials from earlier. She recognized them based on the vibrant color of one. She couldn't make herself look at the other. The question still made no sense to her.

"Options?" she managed to ask.

"The green one will help you. You won't hurt anymore and will finally be at peace... about everything."

"How?"

"It will end your suffering." He unscrewed the lid on it and kneeled down beside her face. "This is the best option."

"I'll be okay then?"

Quinn stared at her behind his glasses.

Lauren sat up with his assistance as he brought it to her lips. "This is the end."

He tipped it up allowing it to hit her lips, but fear caused her to keep her mouth shut. The green liquid ran down her chin numbing the pain in its wake. That's when the truth began to seep in. It wasn't a cure. There was no cure.

Quinn stood up, shaking his head. "You've made your choice."

The heat immediately came back as her screams pierced the air.

"Lauren, damn it!" Taylor shouted.

Her eyes blinked open taking in his severe expression before she turned to the side and began to vomit blood. The tightness in her stomach only seemed to squeeze tighter causing a mixture of noises between a deep moan and a disturbing rumble in her chest. Her veins scorched with a searing she'd never known to exist.

86

Taylor tried using the freezing cold rag to cool her face, and all she could do was groan at the feel of it before she vomited further. The flux of temperatures was both enjoyable and torturous. Lauren was barely dry heaving when she finally lay back onto her bedding, spent of energy.

"Put this in your mouth," he ordered.

The ice cube shone in the candlelight, but the energy it took to accept it failed her. Taylor tugged down her chin and shoved in the cube impatiently. The cube stung blissfully as she closed her eyes, focusing on the coldness. When it melted fully, she opened her eyes with one thought in mind.

"Vials..." Lauren knew they were in her purse. The options were limited, and in the pain she was in, seemed obvious. Could she really make that choice? Was she strong enough? Still with thoughts turning, she pointed to her bag. Taylor brought it closer and rifled through it until he found them. He pulled them out with disgust and conflict.

He offered her the beautiful Mediterranean green vial first. Even as she suffered, it was almost tragically poetic that this was so easy. She wouldn't have to explain it to him. He would just assume that she didn't make it. She still might not.

Lauren stared at the vial in her hand. How simple it was to think of her impending death. The day before, the thought would have been so outrageous. Hours could change so much.

Would it be as peaceful as Quinn said it would be? That seemed to be the only real question. Could she trust Quinn? Why should she?

When she looked at Taylor's hand still holding the vial of blood, a painful shudder wracked her body. She was terrified of being left alone and horrified of having to put him through this. Would she be more of a coward for sending him away? Would she be stronger for the decision?

"Taylor..."

He looked into her eyes then, with a compassion he'd never extended before, stating with certainty, "We will get through this. I'm here."

If she hadn't felt like crying before, she wanted to wail now. Here she was on her deathbed with no positive end in sight, and here he sat, helping her through this. It was then that she realized that her thoughts were getting easier. She could think through the heat. There was a lightness that made thinking faster, simpler...

Panic sped up her breath as she heard Quinn's words repeating back to her. She was making adjustments. She was turning faster.

"Time?" she asked Taylor.

"It's ten o'clock."

There were still hours left? She groaned, deeply uncomfortable with the sizzling heat that was concentrated at her legs and feet. Her toes flexed as zingers ran through each one after descending down her calves. Could she handle four more hours of this?

"I wasn't thinking," Taylor began, placing a cold cloth to her forehead. "We should have put you in a cold bath."

"We both wouldn't fit—"

Her eyes bulged at the words. Not at the implication but the truth of it. She couldn't find her voice. She couldn't find her breath. It was all so excruciatingly clear. She was being taken care of. She was suffering... alone.

Taylor kept silent as he dipped the cloth back into the bowl of ice water. Wasn't she supposed to feel relief that Taylor was fine? She never wanted this to happen to her best friend, but why wasn't she relieved? Was she that selfish?

"Call Quinn," she whispered.

"Lauren, no. You're not thinking clearly."

"Please?" she asked.

He declined as he grabbed another ice cube, putting it in her mouth.

"It's not safe," she mumbled around the cube.

"I know, but... I'm here."

Lauren couldn't find the words to release him from his commitment of staying by her. Loyalty was one of the strongest aspects in their friendship, and it would undo them both if this turned badly. There was no other option.

She glanced at the green-filled vial in her hand again. "Can you get rid of this?"

"What's in it?" he asked, taking it back.

"Suicide in a vial."

"Quinn," he grunted. "He's a dead man."

"It was an option. A peaceful ending."

"And this?" Taylor asked, holding out the blood-filled vial.

"That's a painful existence with a disastrous ending. My future."

Chapter Eight

Lauren was feeling stronger by the minute with the heat merely a buzz in the background. The vial of blood sat on her pillow as she paced around the room. Taylor had left to grab some towels from the car. Her instinct to get up and move was basic after being down for a while.

The smell of blood on the floor that she had expelled was starting to make her nervous. She wasn't repulsed as she should have been. Being trapped around it was only making her insecurities worse.

Taylor breezed back into the room with an armful of towels. He used some of the water from the bowl to dilute the blood and began to wipe it down. The more he scrubbed at it, the stronger the scent perfumed across the room. Her chest was rumbling uncomfortably again.

"I have to get some air," she said, rushing out.

The words merely left her lips as she bolted towards the door. When it swung open, the scents of the night assaulted her causing that rumble to become louder. Something smelled delicious and close, but what restaurant was open this late at night? There wasn't an all-night diner for miles.

Lauren took one step outside of the residence when a hand wrapped tightly around her waist. The shock of the contact caused her to freeze in place. The warm air blew into her ear with distinct orders.

"Get inside," Taylor demanded.

"Can't. Take. Smell," she punctuated.

"I'm working on it. Don't do anything stupid."

Lauren, out of sheer curiosity, wanted to push her limits on his grasp. Certainly, she was stronger than him? However, when she thought about it, it wasn't a great idea. She could accidentally hurt him, and he was there trying to help. She raised her hands palms up, and he released her waist.

She slowly followed his lead back inside, not in any rush to get closer to the mess on the floor. Could she hold her breath until he finished? It was worth a try. She took a slow, deep breath and leaned against the farthest wall. She wouldn't watch him clean up. The noises of the matted towels were enough indication.

Her lungs burned for air and her brain protested the action of closing off the oxygen, but still she held on. There was a desperation within that she couldn't explain. It wasn't until the last possible second that she realized she'd collapse when Taylor's steps inside caught her attention.

"Lauren?"

She took the smallest breath in. The scent was as weak as it was going to get without bleach, an item they never expected to need. When she looked him over, he was missing his sweatshirt.

"How are you feeling?"

"Different," she replied.

"Understatement of the year."

Lauren took a few minutes to focus on the question. She wasn't in physical pain anymore. Her heart was throbbing in her chest like normal, although she could really hear it now. Breathing was still a necessity. Had she really changed at all?

"Do I look different?"

Taylor shook his head. "Is there a chance you didn't fully

convert?"

Lauren grabbed her phone from the bed area. It was one in the morning. There was still time before the eclipse, but what else was there to happen? Her eyes merely glanced at the innocent-looking vial on the pillow.

Quinn had said she would have options. Now that she realized what the first option was, she'd told Taylor to get rid of it. What option was left? Becoming a monster was inevitable. What significance was the blood? Even thinking the word sent a small shudder through her.

"Are you tired?" he asked.

"Not really," she said. "Shouldn't be much longer now, right?"

The words barely left her lips when she suddenly collapsed on the floor. Pain ricocheted throughout her skull, echoing off of the bones. Zings shot through her while she felt the pounding just under her skin. Lauren couldn't even cry out from the pain as slowly but surely blood began to dribble out of the sides of her mouth. A distinct tearing noise sounded in her ears.

Taylor was cautiously standing in front of her. She couldn't be sure if he was talking or not. Everything sounded like chaos, rumbling, crunching, shredding and mind-numbing white noise. Lauren could feel her body trembling as severe pain shot through her jaw, causing the tearing noise to come to the foremost focus. More blood coursed down her chin as she cried out in agony until blackness overcame her.

*****

Lauren sat up in a rush, causing the room to blur. The room

seemed vaguely familiar as she scanned it, taking in the wood-paneled walls and melted down candles. She had been lying down on her bedding. She hadn't been alone, though.

The room was eerily silent with no movement. She got up, noticing the drops of blood across the floor. Pieces of the glass bowl holding the water and ice were scattered; the cloth was missing completely. What could have happened? Where was Taylor?

Lauren ran to the door, but it was blocked in from the outside. She pushed and pushed, but made minimal progress. Why was she blocked in? Her memories were fuzzy from the night before. Her phone began ringing back by the bedding, and she blurred over to it.

"Taylor? Where are you?"

"Is it really you?" he asked.

"Of course it's me. Who else...?"

"Give me a minute," he said as she heard a vehicle engine starting up. After a few seconds, he was pulling open the door cautiously. He looked very serious, and from the way he stood in the doorway, she could tell his shoulders were bunched up with tension.

"Did something happen?"

Taylor looked at her, even further perplexed. "You don't remember?"

Lauren shook her head, noticing the drops of blood trailing to the doorway. "Were we attacked?"

Taylor nodded, still not making a move in her direction. That's when she noticed the cut on his cheek. It was only small, although the bright pink color caught her eye. Her anger started to roll in like tides.

"Who did this to you?" she seethed.

"It was my own fault. I was warned—"

"Warned!" she yelled.

"Lauren, calm down. I'm all right. It's you I'm concerned about."

He must have been kidding. They were attacked, he was hurt, and he wanted her to be calm? All she could think of was someone coming after them. The anger was still rolling in even though she could see his injury was minor.

"Do you need to break something?"

"What?" she asked, perplexed.

"Last night, something triggered your anger. I've never seen anything like it. You almost bit my head off. Instead, you grabbed the glass bowl and shattered it into pieces," Taylor said pointing to his cheek. "You warned me to get back."

Her jaw dropped at the explanation. She was the reason he was hurt. "That doesn't explain that," Lauren said pointing to the tiny drops of blood leading out of the door.

"That's not mine," he replied. "Are you sure you don't want to break anything?"

"Maybe your face if you don't start making sense."

Taylor grunted in response. "I don't think this is going to work. You can't go around threatening people just because you're frustrated. And after last night, you're not very safe to be around."

"Did I come after you? Is that why?"

"I wish that was the reason," he stalled, looking back towards the car. "Maybe you should stay here today. I can come back tonight—"

"You want to leave me here? All alone?"

"Lauren, no one knows you're here. You'll be safe here."

She looked back inside with disgust. It was a disaster area after the broken glass and blood. There was no way she could stay cooped up by herself. When she looked back towards her best friend, his confidence was building in the decision. How long would she be forced to stay in hiding here? Would she ever be allowed back into society?

"Okay..." she whispered hesitantly.

"We can go out when I get back. Rest up."

Lauren nodded, staring at the dried droplets on the floor.

"You really don't remember?" Taylor asked.

"No."

Taylor gave her a strange look but nodded and shut the door behind him, leaving her to ponder what might have happened.

Lauren scrubbed the room clean to the best of her ability with the limited supplies. The droplets of blood that he denied belonging to him must have then belonged to her. It was the only obvious conclusion to draw. Had she tried to escape? Was that why she was inside and he was outside? No wonder he was so cautious around her.

She paid no attention to the time, although the filtering sunlight hinted to the late afternoon. When she finally lay down in her bedding, the sun was setting. She wasn't tired, only contemplative as time inevitably passed her by.

She ran her hand over her arm, feeling the warmth reassure her of who she was. It was the 'what' part that set off the chills. Was she still considered human at all? Maybe not to Fallon or Quinn, but she still had her wits about her.

Her stomach grumbled a complaint, sending a soft rumble from her chest. She hadn't eaten in so long that it was barely a thought. Now it had caught up to her, but what options were there? She was so unprepared for this new condition. Where was the research material that they'd collected?

She searched through the contents of her duffle bag but it had nothing of use. Taylor had taken his things with him when he left. She looked to her phone, sitting eerily silent. Not a single text message awaited her; no one even realized that she was gone. Would she be able to go back to her old life?

Lauren knew the answer was no, but how she ached for the chance to go back to her dorm to live with Hilary and Gina. To be right on campus and get up ten minutes before class. Now it appeared she was a commuter of a different variety.

She thumbed through her cell phone and dialed before her decision to do so became clear. The phone rang and rang until finally being sent to the voicemail. There was no point in leaving a message. Just her call alone would be enough. A few moments later, her phone came to life.

"You're alive?"

"I guess so," she replied.

"And you called me?"

"It wasn't my first choice, but yes, I did. I'm sure you'll be gunning for me now."

Quinn sighed roughly into the line. "Where are you?"

"I'm safe, not that you care. Thanks for asking."

"Lauren—"

"I need a quick education. Do you think you can provide this without trying to murder me?" she asked.

"I wouldn't need to end you. Just as long as you don't become a problem."

"And how do I stay off of the problem list?" Lauren inquired snippily.

"Don't attack humans."

"Why on earth would I want to do that?"

"Wow," Quinn said, perplexed. "You've got no clue, do you?"

"Duh. That's why I called. Why else would I out myself?"

"You haven't eaten then?" he asked.

"That would mean that I knew what I could eat? I've been throwing up everything for the last day. My appetite has been non-existent for so long."

"Since the attack?" he questioned.

"Yeah."

"Where are you?" Quinn asked this time with more interest.

"Nowhere you'll ever think to look. Now, can you please tell me?"

"Where's the vial of blood I gave you?" he asked.

Lauren looked back to her bed, but the vial was gone. She quickly searched around her, but it was nowhere to be found. She thought back to when she was cleaning and remembered no sign of it. What happened to it?

"Lauren?"

"It... it was here, but I can't find it now," Lauren said.

"You... lost... it?"

"It was gross and freaking me out. I remember hiding it and then getting rid of the other vial. I don't remember tossing the blood away, but I could have hidden it again. It's so disgusting. Why did you give me that?" she asked.

"Disgusting? Lauren, you're messing with me now, right?"

Two things happened at the same time. The obvious food issue smacked her in the face. While her mind tried to process that realization, another thought came to mind. "It was your blood, wasn't it?"

"I couldn't offer you death on one hand without life on the other. Regardless of our past, I would never want anything bad to happen to you. I'm not stupid enough to think that you'd have accepted a peace offering of that kind," Quinn admitted.

"Why don't I want to drink your blood?"

"A good question that I don't have an answer for," he admitted.

"Actually, it's not just your blood. I threw up quite a bit of blood last night and… it was all just really awful. I had to clean it all up right away."

"Really? That's pretty amazing, Lauren."

"Amazing!? Have you gone mad?"

"Think about it. The one thing that Sanguis Bellators crave, the one thing that they exist for, their only desire… and you're repulsed by it. Fascinating," Quinn marveled. "You're not hungry at all?"

"I didn't say that. My stomach is grumbling, and I have no idea what to do now."

"Listen to your instincts. It's the only way you'll survive," he stated.

"What if my instincts are to hurt someone? I couldn't let that happen. It's so…"

"The fact that we're having a civilized conversation right now is astounding. The fact that you still care at all about leading a normal life speaks volumes, Lauren."

Her heart began to beat a little faster at his words. Was there hope that she could still lead a normal life? Was it even possible?

"Does that mean I'm different? That maybe I'm not—"

"You're more dangerous to us because of it. Don't kid yourself into thinking you can just come back like everything is back to normal. If you don't feed, you won't make it," he said matter-of-factly.

"What?"

"You need to feed to survive. And if you don't…" he spoke so low it was barely a whisper, "you'll fade away."

Chapter Nine

Time was a lost concept, based on an existence where it needed to be planned accordingly. What was the point of keeping track of time when your condition changed? Was this yet another concept she had yet to understand? As she continued to walk along the side of the road, the darkness of the night only encouraged her passage.

After speaking with Quinn, she was too nervous to be around Taylor. It was bad enough that her temper was so foul. How would she go on, knowing she'd actually done something horrific like attack him? He meant so much to her that the knowledge gave her a cramp. She wouldn't survive this.

Time passed quietly as she journeyed down the road. With her phone turned off, she no longer had to worry about hurting her best friend. It was a smart move seeing how swift her movements could be. She could only imagine his panic when he found the room clean and empty.

A building in front of her with an unusual roof broke through her thoughts. The roof's slant was very severe, and she noticed a few glints upon it from the stars in the sky. As she approached the two-story building, a tiny flame from a hanging lantern beckoned her attention. Her fingers delicately caressed the iron decor in wonder.

"Beautiful, isn't it?"

Lauren stepped back, tugging her hand away. "I'm sorry."

"Oh, dear, don't be. It is a magnificent piece of artistry. Made in the late 1800s," said the older woman.

Lauren took in her gray blouse and black cardigan with a delicate swan pinned to it. Her appearance was business casual with her hair clasped in a tight bun and a light dusting of makeup across her cheeks.

"Can I help you?" the woman offered.

Lauren was already shaking her head.

"Are you lost? Most don't venture this way," she continued.

"I'm okay, thank you," Lauren said politely and began to head back to the road.

"Come back if you change your mind."

Lauren nodded as she continued for the road. There was no point in being so close to anyone whom she could potentially hurt. It was safer if she kept moving. She reluctantly looked back towards the old fashioned lantern that had caught her eye. What was it that had encouraged her to get closer?

The soundlessness was only enhanced as the night grew longer. She was far from any highway or back road where any car would travel. Her footsteps were silent along the grass, leaving nothing but her thoughts for company. Her sense of direction was becoming entangled with the environment.

There was no option to go back. Was there some place meant for her? Where did the rest of the monstrosities stay? Her mind twirled without outcome. Could she survive a life without her family and friends? She'd spent almost her entire life with Taylor by her side, would she be okay without him? Would he forget her?

Her fingers blurred in haste as she turned her phone back on. She didn't even have the chance to dial him as his name displayed across the screen. Her emotions clogged her throat as she saw it. Answering the call was only the first step in giving in. It wasn't something that she wanted to do. Deserting Taylor was an intolerable task, even if it was for his own safety.

"Taylor..."

"Where the hell are you?" he demanded.

"I can't be around you. Or anyone."

"I've spent the last two hours searching for you. Shit, Lauren, you can't just disappear like that," he said.

She could hear the words that he refused to acknowledge. "I'm a monster, Taylor."

"You're a bit high strung and can work on your temper tantrums, but I wouldn't go so far—"

"I'm a Sanguis Bellator. I supposedly survive by feeding on beautiful females and..." Lauren couldn't think of more. Just knowing that she'd have to attack people in order to survive turned her off of the entire thing. She hadn't bothered trying to investigate anything else. "My human life is over."

"If that were true, you wouldn't have answered my call."

The feelings she experienced around him had always brought her comfort. Even if he was frustrated with her. He wouldn't have been frustrated if he hadn't cared. Was it as simple as that? No one knew about what they'd gone through together. He would be the only one who truly knew her before and after the attack.

"Lauren, we can figure something out. Come back," he pled.

"I can't go back to campus. I've been warned," she admitted.

"Fuck Quinn. You can if—"

"I haven't fed, Taylor. I have no real urge to but if it... if I hurt someone—"

"You wouldn't. I know you. If you were capable of hurting

102

someone, it would have been me last night," he said.

"Still, I can't risk it. And I can't stay in that cabin anymore."

"We'll figure it out. I promise you. Just come back," he said.

Lauren could feel her will bending at his request. She didn't want to put people in danger, but maybe there was a compromise? She refused to answer him. She simply hung up the phone and began the trek back.

*****

Her car sat in the parking lot in front of the cabin. She stopped just at the curb with second thoughts. Could she find the will to leave if things became dangerous? She liked to think so, but there had to be more confirmation than hope. There was only one other option, and Taylor would hate it. She made the phone call to verify possibilities before reaching out to her friend.

She refused to go inside, deciding to call him outside. Taylor was surprised by the expression on his face that she'd actually returned, although he tried his best to hide it. She sat on the hood of the vehicle gesturing for him to stop a few feet back.

"I'm not going back to campus without a plan. And you can't guarantee anything. So I'm bringing in the one person who cares more about others than me."

"If you say Quinn, Lauren, I swear I'm going to lose it," Taylor stated.

Lauren smiled just the same. "He has an idea that will protect others and hopefully not kill me."

"Hopefully? Are you not hearing your own words!?"

"Do you want me to stay or not? This could be the only chance, AND it still might not work."

"I can't guarantee that I won't break his face," Taylor said. Lauren got off of the car with her eyes headed down the road away from campus. "Don't give me that. He tried to kill you, Lauren."

Lauren said nothing as she gathered her duffle bag straps and threw it into the vehicle. She hadn't forgotten what Quinn was capable of. If anything, that caused further relief in knowing he'd take every precaution for the benefit of the campus. That was something she couldn't depend on with Taylor.

Taylor got behind the wheel as she slid into the front passenger side seat. She let the window down to allow the smell of the night air to clear her mind and suppress her fears. Had it only been one day? She felt no exhaustion or need to rest.

Taylor kept the radio turned down low, his eyes scanning the outside world for any reason to turn the car around. She wasn't imagining the strong grip he had on the wheel the closer they approached the campus. Deciding to save herself the anxiety of walking across campus to the old building, she had him pull into a closer parking lot.

"Isn't this condemned?" Taylor asked, staring at the decrepit building.

"He'll be here. She will be, too. Be ready."

Lauren left her duffle in the backseat just in case they needed to make a quick escape. She couldn't hear anything out of the ordinary as she carefully entered the building. The main floor was a disaster, but last time she was here, she had the help of the sunlight to guide her. She took her time and helped Taylor duck where part of the ceiling had fallen down.

Her instincts told her to proceed with caution and as silently as possible. The only issue was that sneaking up on Quinn and Fallon could only cause further alarm, not to mention Taylor's heavy footsteps broadcasting their arrival. It wasn't until she reached the top of the crumbling stairs that she spoke up.

"Quinn, are you down there?"

There was no response except for a squeaky noise every few seconds. The sound of shuffling paper was noticeable, too. Lauren glanced over her shoulder at Taylor who was checking their surroundings.

"Quinn?" Lauren asked again, but received no response. "I'm not going to break my neck going down these stairs if you won't even bother answering me."

"He can't hear you," Fallon stated from behind them.

Lauren could barely see her in the dark, standing by the exit. Her silhouette was disrupted by the shadows of the broken room around them. She wouldn't have noticed her at all had she not spoken up.

"He tunes out everything when he is into his work," Fallon continued. "I'm surprised you showed up after the way you left..."

Lauren ignored her comment. "Come on."

Taylor followed her down the stairs as she made her way to the chemistry room. Quinn was elbows deep in papers with a pen behind one ear and a pencil behind the other. His black hair was disheveled by his goggles shoved back on his forehead as he skimmed through a book.

She sat on a stool, waiting for him to finish what he was doing. Unfortunately, Taylor wasted no time, standing beside her and loudly slamming his hands against the lab table. In a startled jumble, Quinn dropped his book to the floor.

"Oh... I-I didn't hear you come in."

"Find anything helpful?" Lauren asked.

"I'm still looking into it. I've been trying to work out a cure for years now with no luck. Trying to curb your appetite might be all that I need to do," he explained.

"Is that easier?"

"Nothing about this is easy, Lauren. It takes work, dedication—"

"So you can't do it," Taylor interrupted.

"I didn't say that. It's going to take time to figure out."

Fallon leaned against the doorframe. "What was the last thing you ate?"

Lauren shrugged. "I had cranberry juice, I think."

Quinn stared at Lauren in awe. "I need a sample from your veins."

Lauren wasn't a fan of needles. It seemed odd that even now the thought of it made her stomach queasy. Quinn removed a long syringe from one of the drawers in addition to an alcohol wipe. Her hands gripped into fists at her sides as she glanced toward the exit. Fallon was still lounging against the frame like part of her knew that this would be an issue.

"There's no other way?"

Quinn grimaced with the shake of his head. "Close your eyes and take a deep breath."

Lauren looked to Taylor as she reluctantly offered her left arm. It wouldn't hurt that bad, she kept trying to convince herself. Her friend was little to no help at all. He was too busy staring daggers at Quinn and over-analyzing his every movement.

Lauren felt the pressure of the needle a split second before the pinch. She squeezed her eyes shut as he filled up two tubes worth of liquid. When he removed the needle from her arm, she felt lightheaded and leaned heavily against the table.

"Is two enough?" Fallon asked, coming to Quinn's side.

"Don't have much of a choice," he replied, nodding to Lauren's slumped form.

"Great," Fallon said sarcastically.

"Now what?" Taylor asked impatiently.

"You can rest for now. I'll let you know what I come up with," Quinn said. "Where are you staying?"

Lauren shrugged weakly. She was only thinking of the very next step. And in this moment, nothing was that important.

Taylor stood up with purpose. "Don't worry about it."

"She's dangerous," Fallon stated.

"You don't know anything about her." Taylor leaned against the table, challenging Fallon.

Quinn shook his head. "Taylor, I understand how you feel. It doesn't change the facts." As confirmation of his words, he held up the tube filled with her blood. It was thick and black, like tar.

*****

107

"Can you make it up the stairs?"

"I'm not helpless," she complained.

Taylor ignored her as he grabbed her duffle bag and went up the stairs. She followed quietly, fighting the urge to take a quick nap on the stairs. Any danger she might have posed felt like a joke now. Taylor could probably kill her by accident; she was just too tired to think any further.

He didn't hesitate going right into the dorm room, shutting the door behind her. What did surprise her was Jeff's side of the room filled with her belongings from her dorm room. Her bedspread and pillows were the most shocking, not to mention the few minuscule items from her desk on top of the usually empty one.

"What is this?"

"You were worried about hurting people, especially ones who you care about. I suspected attacking Hilary would be mostly on your mind since she has been getting under your skin," he explained.

"So you moved me in here?"

"At least I know what to expect from you," he said, kicking off his shoes.

Lauren rolled her eyes. He thought he knew, but even she was clueless. She could only hope that Quinn would figure something out to make her existence easier, if there were a chance of that happening at all. Reading could only do so much.

"This is incredibly..." Lauren wasn't sure what to finish with: stupid, insane, careless?

"Yeah, yeah, don't go getting all sappy on me now. Just get some rest, and we can devote the weekend to making this work," he said.

Chapter Ten

Lightning woke her abruptly causing her to sit straight up in bed. Her blond mane blocked her view only heightening her anxiety. Even the sight of Taylor slumbering across the room wouldn't tame it. The crash of thunder sent her to the window in a blur.

"I don't think I'll get used to that," he commented, watching her from his bed.

"To what?"

"How fast you are," he said.

Lauren stared out the window, watching the downpour soak the campus. The grounds were empty except for one or two students running from building to building. The proximity of other people was a huge risk that wasn't warranted. She had to leave.

"Where's my keys?"

"Why?" he asked.

"Why do I want to know the location of my property?" Lauren asked sarcastically.

"Did I forget something?"

"No..."

Taylor rolled away from her. "Good."

"My car keys, Taylor."

She watched him lie there like he hadn't heard her. She looked at the desk again, taking in the minor details. He had placed everything just as she had, like he'd memorized it. Her laptop sat in the middle while her lamp of clear crystals and gold design shimmered on the left side. Even her notepad sat with her favorite bulky pen awaiting her attention.

Lauren sat on the edge of her presumed bed, running her hand up and down her arm. When a sore spot caused a wince, she stopped, taking care to look at her left arm. It was where Quinn had taken her blood. Was it blood? Her naivety about her current condition wasn't helping her feel any less anxious.

She glanced around her area, noticing the stack of books. The ones she borrowed from the library had to still be there. She certainly hadn't returned them. Her fingers traced over the bindings, picking out the book before setting it on the bed.

Thumbing through the pages with her new, clearer vision helped quite a bit. She could tell the difference more quickly between the inserted pages, jotting down the information in her notebook to refer to afterward. When she completed that, she went to Taylor's side of the room, careful not to wake him again. Taking the scanned papers and putting them together could only accomplish so much. There were huge gaps that needed to be filled.

The time on her phone read about nine in the morning. The library was open, and with any sort of luck, still empty for the most part. With eyes closed, Lauren took stock of her feelings, she felt as calm as she possibly could with everything going on. She felt determined to find more information about what was happening to her. But her most vital concern while on campus was one of being hungry, and that was easily answered. Breakfast wasn't something she participated in normally, and it was a pleasant surprise to see that that had applied to this new way of life too. Well, as pleasant as it would get anyway.

She quietly grabbed a change of clothes, showered and took off to the one place that might have the answers she'd been looking for. Even in the early hours of the library, she knew to slip in through the lesser-used door and researched in the least used area in the building.

Hours later, she returned back to the dorm loaded down with papers. Taylor buzzed her in before she ascended the stairs and into the room.

"You wouldn't believe—"

"Where have you been?" Taylor asked.

"Oh, at the library. We started doing the research, but still I needed to know more. There's so much information here, I couldn't even read it all. I just scanned and scanned..." Lauren glanced up to his worried face. "What?"

"You didn't hear?"

"Obviously not... What is it?" she questioned.

Taylor stood in front of the door with a grimace. "Last night, there was an attack on campus."

Lauren could only whisper in shock. "What?"

"A freshman was found disoriented in the parking lot..."

Lauren couldn't find the words to speak. Her eyes squinted as she turned away, trying to hide her emotions. She cupped her mouth as she leaned against the bed. Someone else was attacked on campus. A freshman, for goodness sake!

"Are... they okay?"

"The rumor is she's in critical condition," Taylor stated.

A scream from the bottom of her stomach begged to be released. A loud guttural rumble penetrated out; she clasped her mouth to keep from vomiting. Another victim was taken against her will. A perfect stranger to Lauren, but it didn't change how she felt. She knew what it felt like to be attacked and could only imagine how horrific of an ordeal it felt like for the freshman.

"Lauren, it's not your fault that this happened."

"Do you think Quinn—"

The sound of her phone began to shriek, cutting off her sentence. Taylor glared at her in response like she'd conjured his existence with her words. She took a deep breath and reached for the phone. She answered hesitantly, not bothering to speak. What was there to say?

"Where are you?" Quinn demanded.

"I was researching..." She took another breath. "I just heard..."

"Were you on campus last night?"

Fear shot through her just as quickly as the adrenaline did. "I didn't do this. I would never—"

"Answer the damn question, Lauren. Were you here?"

"I was with Taylor last night. Why?"

"I need confirmation from you that you didn't step foot on this campus after you left our meeting last night. It's the only way to keep Fallon from coming for you. She's convinced you did it," he said. "Bellators can't be trusted."

The silence was deafening over the line. If she told the truth, it was all over. Even as a Bellator, she had no real fighting skills. She'd have to run away and never come back, and that would be confirmation enough that she'd done it. She was more than a hundred percent positive that she'd been in bed all night long.

Lauren muted the line, facing Taylor straight on. "Would you lie

113

for me?"

"What about?"

"Would you lie to save my life, Taylor?" she pushed.

He nodded slowly, giving her a glare.

Lauren unmuted the phone line. "Quinn, I spent the night off campus with Taylor. We were occupied for most of the evening."

Silence answered her for a few seconds. Then Quinn quietly replied, "Oh."

Ignoring his weak response, she pushed forward. "I'm on campus now trying to research. We have to find a way to protect people. No one deserves to be like this."

"Yeah, well, I'm working on it. Let me calm Fallon down so that I can get back to it."

The phone line went dead in her hands. When she looked up, Taylor's glare had changed into disapproving revulsion.

"You said you'd lie..."

"To save your life. What does that have to do with us being 'occupied'? You know what he thinks now," he said.

"I don't know what he thinks, and I don't care. Fallon was milliseconds from coming after me. I don't wanna... just fade away."

Lauren glanced out the window, willing her fear to calm down. Strong arms wrapped around her waist, tugging her back into a muscular chest. His warm breath brushed the back of her neck. Rain pelted the window, dripping down the glass as if the sky were representing her inner emotions.

"You have nothing to fear. You're a Bellator. You could take her if you had to," he said.

"No, you've never seen her."

"And you haven't even tried to protect yourself. I get that you don't want to hurt anyone, but you can't let anyone else get you, either," he said.

"I know."

"I won't say anything about you being here last night, but this isn't the time for you to leave. Just stay here, and I'll cover for you," Taylor said. "I'll clear the air with Quinn, too. He probably thinks that I bagged you."

Lauren shoved him off. "Eww. Who even talks like that?"

Taylor smirked. "I do. Now, what did you find out?"

"Help me get this together in the right order, and we can both figure it out," she said, pointing to the scanned papers on her bed.

*****

Taylor agreed to take the original books back to the library that Lauren had taken out. She didn't want to risk bumping into Fallon for any unneeded reason. Instead, she decided to stay safe and dry in the dorm room.

The sound of her phone going off merely jostled her as she answered it, only realizing too late that she shouldn't have. "Hey, Collin."

"Hey there, stranger. What happened to you on Thursday?"

Lauren had completely forgotten about the midterm for Historic Theatre. "Um… something came up."

"Is Klein going to let you take it?" he asked.

115

"I think so, but I won't know until next week. What's going on?" Lauren asked, wanting to get him off the phone.

"You're still coming tonight, right?"

"Tonight... the kegger..." She thought it through for a second. "I don't know... I'm freaked about the attack on campus last night."

"That's why you should come. Everyone needs a stiff drink," he encouraged.

"Oh... I don't—"

"Just one drink. I'll see you tonight," he said before hanging up.

Lauren closed her eyes, trying to shove Collin out of her mind. She didn't need another thing to worry about. She paper-clipped the papers together and slid them into her backpack before swinging it over her shoulder. After locking up the dorm door, she blurred down the stairs.

She waited in the lobby, pacing in the small area, until her eyes caught something in the window—a shadowy figure, obscured by the heavy downpour. The drops of water pelted her face as she found herself outside, suddenly drawn toward it without explanation. The light brown jacket hung over broad shoulders tapering down to dark pants and boots. The jacket's collar was popped up, gently caressing the dark, chin length hair.

Lauren's eyes focused on the stern face that seemed familiar and foreign all at once. His face was smooth, apart from the furrowed brow that darkened his brown eyes. She was a mere ten yards from the compelling stranger when she was stopped short with firm hands on her shoulders. When she looked up into the familiar eyes of Taylor, her

116

stupor seemed to wear off.

"You're soaked. What are you doing out here?" Taylor asked, walking her under the shelter of the dorm roofing.

"I... don't know?"

"You're saying that a lot lately. Losing brain cells as a Bellator?" he joked.

"Taylor!" she hissed, looking back to the figure, but no one was there. "Where'd he go?"

"Who?"

"That man... I thought I might have known him. Maybe saw him in passing?" she stated and questioned all at once.

"Like who?"

Lauren shrugged, unsure. "Quinn's waiting."

They made their way to the now all too familiar, deteriorating building. The floor had spots of puddles and mud as they carefully stepped around debris. Taylor went down the stairs first with her following his lead. There was an eerie silence once her feet touched the bottom step of the stairs.

Taylor reached out for the door handle of the lab as Lauren grabbed his other arm, warning him with a pressured grip. She was seen as the enemy here. Her word meant nothing, and if Fallon decided to attack her, she wouldn't want Taylor to get hurt in the mix, trying to protect her. She didn't have to ask him to know that he would.

"Let me..." she encouraged, trying to get around him.

"Lauren—"

"I'm faster than you are. Trust me," she said, pushing her way in front of him and opening the door.

Quinn sat with his hands folded on the tabletop like he was patiently awaiting her arrival. Her eyes scanned the room, taking in that he was alone. Taylor was right behind her with every step inside the room.

"Fallon's not here," Quinn said.

"If she thinks I'm a threat, then why not?"

"She still does, even when I tried to plead your case. I'm sorry about that. So I told her I was busy, so she left," Quinn stated. "I hope that I made the right choice in believing you."

"I'm not a threat, but we do have a problem. I think there was another Bellator on campus today."

"Other than you…"

"He was staring at me from afar, and I… was drawn to him," she admitted softly, lowering her eyes.

"Drawn? Like instinctively?" Quinn asked.

Lauren suddenly wished she'd chosen another word to use. "I just wanted to see—"

"And you? Did you see him?" Quinn asked Taylor.

"No. I was too distracted by the rain to pick up anything weirder than her standing in it blatantly," Taylor said.

"What are you thinking?" Lauren asked Quinn, openly worried.

"I should have thought of it. Expected it… This is my error," Quinn stated as he stared directly at her. "It's because of you. The attack on campus last night and Fallon's increased sightings."

"Me? I didn't do anything!" Lauren shouted, frustrated.

"Exactly. *You're not doing anything.* You're not feeding, you're not attacking people, and you're not even trying to be like one of them. You're… unique and coveted," he said, his eyes darting back and forth between her and Taylor.

"Listen, about that—" Taylor began.

"I've noticed minor changes, but nothing this serious, Quinn. You think they're coming after me?" Lauren said, cutting off Taylor.

"Lauren, you're very intriguing. The company you keep doesn't fluctuate, you keep to yourself as well as being overly compassionate to those around you. I can sympathize with your struggle in transitioning into a Bellator, but those attributes are most likely why you were targeted."

Lauren was at a loss for words.

"Do you even know how many attacks have taken place on this very campus over the last four years?" Quinn asked. "At least three a year that I've learned, but it's already been three in the first semester this year. That's very unusual."

"What does that have to do with Lauren?" Taylor asked.

"Everything. Can't you see? The first attack was to turn you, Lauren. The second woman that you just 'happened' to walk upon was a test," Quinn advised.

"I helped them…" Lauren whispered. "The woman and Fallon."

Slowly, the pieces were starting to come together, one by one. The Bellators figured that her cravings would have kicked in to feed on the defenseless woman while they distracted Fallon. They were not prepared for her to actually help either one of them. She'd failed the test in two different ways at once.

"Last night was another test…"

"Why else do you think the freshman survived it? Do you know how easy it is for a student to disappear, especially on this large of a campus? Who's going to notice?" Quinn said.

Pressure collected upon her shoulders, encouraging her take a seat at the lab table. Her very existence consisted of putting innocent people at risk whether she was on campus or not. While lying to Quinn to get Fallon off of her back was important, she could only hope it wouldn't come up to bite her in the long run.

She slid the backpack off of her shoulder, allowing it to sit on the table before her. The pressure was accumulating with every second as she thought through the next step. This was more than just about her life; this was a bigger problem than she had ever imagined it could be. She'd have to let him in...

"Quinn, I'm going to ask you a question. It's simple. Yes or no. The consequences to your answer will weigh heavily on which answer you decide to choose," she said, staring him down.

Quinn folded his hands again on the tabletop and nodded.

"Can I trust you, unconditionally, for better or for worse, without question or deceit?"

His eyes widened at the question. She watched his face as he thought it through. She understood his hesitation, taking into consideration a possible fallout with Fallon, the impending danger into which he'd be directly put and the amount of work that would come with this. Whether he wanted to be part of this or not, he had only been helping Fallon on the side. This was his decision to make and his alone.

"Trust isn't given, it's earned," he replied.

"As far as I can tell, you've been on the right track since I was attacked. There's a great deal more I'd be willing to share if I had your word that you would stand by me. I don't expect you to choose between Fallon and me. I know where I stand."

"In the name of science, I agree to stand by you. That is all I can promise," Quinn said.

Lauren nodded, accepting his terms and reading between the lines. She pulled out the papers and set them on the table. She watched him skim through the pages with minimal interest before pushing them back to her.

"I've read this all before. This would be more of a benefit to you both. Learn what you're truly capable of and what the life of a real Bellator is like."

*****

The rain had slowed to a drizzle by the time Lauren and Taylor had made their way out of the dilapidated science building. Taylor had stayed eerily quiet through the conversation with Quinn. As they walked in silence, a growing unease began to creep in. She knew how Taylor felt towards Quinn, and her offering to allow closer proximity was clearly a problem they'd have to work out.

It wasn't until they were back in the dorm room when she noticed his attention on the doorframe. She put her backpack down on the floor beside the bed. He reached into his pocket, pulling out his vibrating cell phone and answering it straight away.

"Hey, Kelsey," he greeted. "Oh, really?"

Taylor's dark eyes flicked her way for a moment. "Yeah, listen, change of venue all right?"

Lauren turned her back on him, kicking her backpack under the bed. She grabbed her purse from the desk and decided to take a trip to the bathroom. Without giving him another look, she walked out of the room and down the hall. It wasn't until she was inside the safety of the bathroom that her lungs tried to break through her ribs.

Her fingers gripped her sides as she hung her head allowing her mangled tresses to cover her face. Thoughts flew through her mind so quickly that nothing surfaced to be remembered. Feelings of uncomfortable invasion rippled through her chest without warrant.

Lauren closed her eyes, breathing in through her nose and out of her pursed lips. When calmness settled in again, she glanced at her reflection in complete horror. She looked a mess with her hair tangled from the rain. Her face was splotchy red across her high cheekbones. It was a mask, hiding the vile creature inside.

She wanted to cry. She wanted to scream and cause physical violence to the one who'd done this to her. There was no question of her desire to not harm others, but could it happen anyway? Was she strong enough to not only protect others but not to be a threat, either? It was one thing believing it and saying it out loud. She wanted to prove it to be true.

She washed her face quickly before putting light foundation on. She settled for a subtle swipe of mascara and eyeliner to brighten her light eyes. She'd always felt better after sprucing up, but the joy was eclipsed by the potentially fatal encounter it could lead to. This was bigger than a test, though. If she could slip back into her old self without anyone else watching, she'd know without a doubt what she was capable of.

After a few minutes, she returned to the dorm room. Taylor was pacing the small area, only to stop, noticing her return. She grabbed her hairbrush from the dresser and made a few passes through her hair to get the tangles out before admiring her reflection. It wasn't great, but better than it had been.

"I'm going out for a while," Taylor said.

"Me, too."

"Oh, yeah?" he questioned.

"Yup," she said, flinging her hair over one shoulder. "See you later."

When she reached the lobby, the uncomfortable feeling started to come back. She wasn't sure what it was from exactly. She glanced outside into the night through the glass doors. Was this discomfort caused from the Bellator being on campus? She gripped her fists and opened the door, traipsing out and onto the sidewalk.

The drizzle had stopped completely allowing the fresh air to cleanse her senses. There was no sign of the guy she'd seen earlier. There were a few students headed towards the cafeteria, laughing loudly in the quiet evening. She remembered what it had been like to laugh like that with her roommates.

She hadn't spoken to them in four days. Had it truly only been that short a time? Her human life had ended miserably, and no one but Taylor seemed to notice in the least. She shook the thoughts out of her mind as she continued ahead towards either her salvation or devastation.

"I'm outside," she said into the phone line not waiting for him to greet her.

"Okay."

It took only a minute for Collin to open the door to allow her entry. He was wearing a dark baseball cap turned backwards with an equally dark t-shirt and jeans. His mouth turned up in the corners at her appearance. She wore a gray shirt with black long sleeve cardigan over dark jeans. She hadn't dressed up like the girls usually did for parties.

"You're early," he said, leading her to his room.

The room was laid out with the beds pushed up against the opposite walls. There was a small couch set beneath the two windows that had the shades pulled down. The desks were pushed against the wall, and she noticed the alcohol sitting on top still in the bags they came in.

Collin grabbed an already open beer can, sipping on it as he waved towards the desk with his other hand. "Grab whatever you'd like."

The options were limited to cheap, watery beer or cheaper vodka. She knew that Tony always brought reinforcements of the better variety later in the evening. Not that she planned on staying that late this evening. That's when it dawned on her. Could she consume alcohol and stay in control? Would her body accept it?

She hadn't peed in days, only needing the bathroom to shower or refresh her face. What had she gotten herself into? Picking up a can of beer, she sat down on the couch while he tapped on his keyboard for a minute. The sounds of house music began to play out of the speakers.

He sat down on the couch, taking another swig of his beer.

"So, why'd you pick Historic Theatre?" she asked.

"Needed another course to graduate. Less painful than anything else offered."

She nodded even though she didn't feel the same way.

"You gonna drink that or watch it?" he asked with a grin.

"I haven't decided yet." She looked at the unappealing can. "So was there a reason you wanted me to come tonight?"

"To party?"

"I've been to a few of your parties and never rated a personal invitation over the phone before." Lauren glimpsed at his overly confident facial expression.

"And you still manage to be here before anyone else, even when you try to get out of it," he said.

She stood up, going back to the desk only to put the can of beer with the rest. Drinking wasn't going to help the current situation in any way. It was a relief that she didn't feel the urge to get closer to Collin. In fact, being across the room felt better and better.

Lauren thought back to when she realized he had some interest in her. It certainly had caused curiosity on her end, but feelings of desire for him, it did not. He was attractive—that wasn't even a good enough word for him. She couldn't put her finger on what she really felt.

The door opened, bringing in Collin's roommate, Gordon, and a handful of people she didn't know. She took slow, deep, calming breaths watching the fellow peers grab beers and claim spots to stand. Her focus was so intent on staying calm that Collin's approach caught her unprepared.

"Lauren, come here," he coaxed, grabbing her hand. "What happened to your beer?"

She laughed nervously. "I don't need liquid courage to talk to you."

"Obviously not," he laughed. "Usually, you loosen up a bit, though. I feel like your gonna quiz me any minute."

"You think I'm pretentious?"

"Not at all," Collin said seriously.

Lauren fidgeted with the sleeve of her cardigan. When she glanced up, more people were piling into the small room. The heat was rising noticeably; however, removing the cardigan wasn't something she wanted to do.

"Lauren? You're here?" Tony asked, finding her leaning against the side of Collin's bed.

"Yeah..."

"You might want to go talk to Hilary outside before she comes in. She's pretty pissed," Tony mentioned.

Collin raised his eyebrow at her in question. She didn't have time to explain, and he didn't really need an explanation in the first place. Lauren stepped out of the small triangle, heading out of the door. Hilary was just walking through the lobby doors when Lauren spotted her with Gina and Max. The glare Hilary sent should have been enough to transport her elsewhere.

"Hey," Lauren greeted.

"Hey? That's all you have to—"

"Hey," Gina said, cutting off Hilary.

"Guys, can we talk?" Lauren asked.

Lauren went over to the couch as Gina followed. Reluctantly, Hilary claimed one of the armchairs, crossing both her legs and arms in protest. Lauren thought through the situation. What could she say? She certainly couldn't open up about everything, but she could still warn them.

"I can understand you both being upset with me."

"I'm not upset, Lauren. I'm worried about you," Gina stated.

Lauren glanced down at her entwined hands. "I'm going to be okay."

"What happened?" Hilary asked.

"I-I can't talk about it." The bottom of Lauren's lip trembled at the words.

Gina placed a gentle hand upon hers. "Lauren, we're here to help. You know you can tell us anything, but I understand that you feel you can't."

Lauren's heart broke at the words. Her emotions were bundling up in her chest causing a chaos effect resulting in shortness of breath. The more she fought for control, the harder it became, like falling apart was an option. She had to focus hard, clearing her throat to get her real message out to them.

"When you're walking around campus, be aware of your surroundings. Try to stay in a group, okay?"

"Yeah, well, with what happened to that freshman—"

"That was only a rumor," Hilary interrupted. "Just a drunk freshman who didn't know their limit."

Lauren's eyes widened, suddenly realizing how easily the truth

127

could be clouded. It would end up like the game of telephone. Who knew the facts when it reached the end? This was worse than she feared. Even if no one knew of the Bellators on campus, it seemed that protecting themselves wasn't a concern. Another case of blaming the victim.

Hilary stood up, eyeing Tony waving her over. "It's party time."

Gina sighed, gesturing to Tony that she needed another minute. Lauren wasn't sure what else there was to say. They both stood from the couch, but Gina put her arms around Lauren, hugging her closely. Lauren hugged her back, wishing it was possible to go back to the night of the football game.

Lauren stepped back with heavy words weighing on her tongue. She glanced towards Tony realizing he was still there waiting for Gina. Hilary had already gone inside with Max. This would be the only chance, and she knew her roommate would listen.

"Gina, it's not safe to go around the campus alone. Please be careful."

Gina nodded, watching Lauren walk towards the lobby doors.

"Lauren?"

Lauren glanced back to Gina who now seemed to be on edge. "Yeah?"

"The attack on the freshman? It wasn't a rumor, was it? It was true."

Lauren nodded solemnly.

"Did it happen to..." Gina asked, eyeing her, unable to vocalize the question.

Lauren couldn't answer her. Her throat had practically sewn itself shut. Instead, she took her leave out of the doors, allowing Gina to decide on her own. It was obvious either way. She could only hope that Gina would take care of Hilary. Lauren now knew she had to remove herself from the human world. She was no longer part of it.

Chapter Eleven

Three days had passed with little to no activity. Quinn was running interference for her with Fallon. While she no longer had to worry about attending classes and passing tests, she still had responsibilities. With a set distance from Fallon, her nights were now filled with patrolling the campus for sightings of Bellators. Fallon would patrol the other side of campus, unwilling to acknowledge any assistance given.

"How are you holding up?" Quinn asked over the phone.

"I'm okay."

"Still no cravings? Hunger pains?" he inquired.

"Nope."

"Hmmm... any new developments?"

"Nothing really. Taylor says my temper is getting worse," she sneered, walking through the campus parking lot.

"Irritability? About what?"

"You'd have to ask him," she said as movement in the shadows caught her attention. "Quick question. If I fed, would it change who I am?"

Alarmed, his voice became focused. "Why? Have you fed?"

"No. The thought alone repulses me. As a scientist, though—"

"Lauren, you're unlike any Bellator I've come across. That doesn't mean that you have a privilege. You've strayed from the basic components of your world. It could mean benefits or disadvantages, but I'm not willing to risk the population unless we had a way to cage you."

Her feet stopped as the shadow ran across the aisle on all fours.

She was stalking a raccoon. This entire idea was hers, but being caged wasn't going to fly. She wasn't a lab rat, and she wasn't going to be treated as one. Even now, it was like she was a convict only allowed out on parole. At least she had some sort of freedom.

"Never," she growled into the line.

"All right, well, there's your answer."

"You'd get a kick out of that wouldn't you?" she asked.

"I'm not trying to be cruel. It would be helpful only as a benefit to help protect the innocent, which I thought we were both trying to do."

"You're not locking me up. End of conversation."

"How's your energy level?" Quinn continued down the list, changing the subject.

"Better, although I don't deep sleep anymore. It's like I'm on the verge of waking up the entire time, but it's enough to feel rested. I can't describe it better than that."

"How long do you sleep for?"

"Ten to twelve hours sometimes..." Her words faltered as she noticed a small light in the distance. Her eyes locked in as her feet drew her closer in determined steps. Her eyesight seemed to strengthen seeing the exact contours of the black iron design. The intricate design of many years ago was calling to her. Her fingers reached out to touch the lantern that hung so delicately from a limb. "Quinn..."

"In the darkest of nights, there is a light that will summon you home," a voice said.

"Quinn..."

"A keepsake until you find your way," the voice whispered from behind her.

Lauren spun around quickly, noticing the figure concealed in the shadows of the trees. Her breath caught as she gripped the phone in her fingers. She blinked a few times trying to determine any type of description, but the form was so ambiguous it was hard to tell.

The words hesitantly sat upon her tongue. She was unsure of the correct thing to do when the figure suddenly blurred out of view. Before she could react, the cold steel pierced her skin, slicing upwards into her rib cage. Her eyes widened at the exquisite pain, her hands automatically dropping the phone and shoving back at the attacker, sending them flying against the side of a vehicle.

Lauren peered down at the blade still plunged inside her. She hesitantly pulled it back out, finding it covered in the black liquid she knew was her new life source. A shiver trembled her entire form as she hugged herself tightly. She took shallow breaths, trying to block out the pain as she prayed that she hadn't been done in.

Loud squawking sounded from her feet as she peered between the phone and the blade. She looked up to find Fallon picking herself up from the cement, noticing the dent against the side of the car. Her chest rumbled deeply sending zings of pain from her wound. Still, she kept her focus on Fallon. Her hands balled into fists as her feet steadied themselves impatiently.

"I knew it. You're not as innocent as you'd like everyone to believe," Fallon grunted.

"You stabbed me."

"Accident," Fallon stated.

"Ditto."

Fallon laughed darkly for a moment before wincing. "Whatever."

Lauren tried to calm herself with a few deep breaths, but any attempt to reign in her anger was slipping through her grasp. "I suggest you be on your way."

"I don't listen to you."

"If you'd like to keep your body intact, you'll listen. I'm losing more than my patience with you," Lauren stated with gritted teeth. "Leave..."

Grasping her side, Lauren barely flinched, noticing the pain had dulled. Her fingers lightly traced the area, taking in that there was no flow of liquid any longer. She waited until she was certain that Fallon had made her way towards the opposite side of the parking lot before picking up her phone.

Quinn had hung up. She didn't want to think about anything he might have heard. As she turned to the tree limb, the lantern hung as witness. Grabbing up the light, she took her time getting back to the room.

Lauren placed the lantern beside her bed. She tugged off her jacket and dropped it over the side of the laundry bin. She went to the mirror, lifting her shirt up to inspect further. There was an angry black line at her ribs that was tender as she brushed her fingertips lightly over it. Her chest began to tighten as the gravity of the situation seeped in.

Her knees gave way, sending her to the floor. She could have died tonight. Accident or not, it was that easy. And no one would be the wiser as to what happened. She didn't believe Fallon in the least, to be honest, if it had come to that. She'd have been portrayed as the aggressor, but still, Lauren was incredibly vulnerable. Maybe Taylor was right. She needed to be able to protect herself.

The sound of the door opening caused her to scramble to her feet. She turned away, grabbing the lantern and pushing it out of sight beside the dresser. She grabbed a clean V-neck t-shirt and clambered out of the room.

A strange tension had materialized between her and Taylor since the night the freshman was attacked. She couldn't put into words what was off between them, and worse, wouldn't. If he had noticed, he didn't feel it important enough to speak about. And if he hadn't noticed, then maybe she was being too sensitive. All things considered, after tonight, she felt it was with cause.

Lauren changed her shirt in the bathroom, making sure to bundle up the shirt ruined with her life source. She was cleaning up the edge of the wound when it began to fade away. Even before her blinking eyes, it faded until it disappeared completely. The comfort of the knowledge that her body healed itself so dramatically was only minimal.

Returning back to the quiet dorm room, she noticed Taylor sitting at his desk. She made her way to the bedside when he cleared his throat. She closed her eyes, hoping that he wouldn't choose now to start up a conversation. The art of talking was currently useless to her.

"This was by the mirror..." he said.

She turned around, noting the switchblade in his hand. If she played it off, maybe it would be okay. Shrugging nonchalantly, she reached out for it as he placed it in her hands. "Thanks. I was looking for it."

"What happened?"

"Nothing. Just routine patrol." She turned her back, putting the ruined shirt in the laundry atop the jacket. That's when she noticed the jacket missing.

"This doesn't look like nothing..." Taylor stated, holding up the jacket.

"You're going through my laundry now?"

He raised his eyebrow, waiting for an answer. Lauren shook her head as she went to her closet, grabbing a hoodie. She tossed it on and threw her hair up in a messy bun, ignoring him. Moving in with him definitely had its disadvantages. He meant well, she knew, but he was a bit much to deal with all of the time.

"I had an accident. No big deal," she said, heading for the door.

She blurred out of the room, not stopping until she was outside. The breeze had taken on a distinct chill, even during the short period of time of being inside. She glanced up at the sky; the twinkling stars betrayed those who were enchanted. Patrolling the campus for the night was her responsibility, and she would do her best not to let anyone get hurt.

*****

The sun had set taking the minimal warmth with it. The chill had turned bitter forcing heavier jackets, colorful scarves and gloves upon the campus. Lauren wrapped her lavender scarf loosely around her neck as she exited the dorm. The cool weather seemed to affect her less than her peers; the coolness was mildly annoying and barely registered.

She walked the campus grounds, keeping an eye out for anything out of the ordinary. Her instincts kept her from straying too far from the well-lit path. The Bellators moved fluidly, with purpose, using the cover of darkness and distraction to their advantage. It wasn't that difficult to understand.

As she passed by the art history building, her eyes took in the grand archway. It always called to her prior to the change, but now she really longed to be part of it.

"Ms. Benson?"

Her heart began to race—only one person acknowledged her that way. Professor Klein was walking up the path towards the building. His hair had been cut down neatly on the sides, allowing the length on top to be easily brushed back. Was it even possible for him to appear more handsome?

"Hello, Professor," she replied. "You're here late."

"I forgot my workbook on the podium."

Lauren nodded as burning guilt rushed through her veins. What more was she to say? Was there something she *should* say? She ran a hand through her hair nervously as he reached for the door.

"Would it be a waste of time to explain my absence?"

"Typically? Yes," he said, holding the door open behind him. "Since I'm already behind, though, you may try while I retrieve my workbook."

Lauren glanced up to his open expression as his dimples subtly hinted a possible smile awaiting. Following his trail inside, she felt a rush of anxious energy bombard her just walking through the familiar halls.

"Well?"

"A great deal has changed in the last few weeks. Fears that I've never had before..." Lauren paused, trying to wrap her mind around it. "Nowhere is safe anymore."

Professor Klein opened the door to the classroom, waving her inside. "Times have changed. I can attest to that."

She was unsure as to what to say. He went about collecting his items, placing them inside his messenger bag.

"I was asked if life imitates art or vice versa. I would have to agree that art imitates life. It only captures the most beautiful pieces life has to offer."

"Beauty is in the—"

"No one would see beauty in what I've endured..." Her tone had started off as stern only to falter in the end. She refused to look up at her professor. Embarrassment warmed her chest at even trying to explain. Her human life was over. She knew that, but part of her didn't want to let go. She just wanted things to go back like they were.

"The ones who can see are the only ones who matter, Lauren," he said, coming to stand before her. "If you want others to appreciate what beauty we have here in front of our faces, you have to try. Are you willing?"

"Yes," she answered.

"Okay, then. I expect you here on Thursday for class. After class ends, I will allow you to take the revised midterm," Professor Klein said before turning to walk out of the classroom, leaving her slack-jawed in his wake.

Chapter Twelve

There was no stopping her once Professor Klein gave her a chance. She went around to her courses, discussing her dilemma with minimal detail and heavy overcasting. Her professors were willing to have her continue as a student, but only two allowed her to retake the midterms. That meant she would be overwhelmed with studying until she was back on track.

When Thursday evening came, she had her backpack loaded with everything she'd need. She left her room early, wrapped up snugly— not because she was cold but rather to fit in. The frost was glazing the grass and outdoor landmarks alluding to the season's transformation.

She was the first to enter the classroom as she was in the past. Her backpack sat in the empty chair beside her as she tugged out her notebook, waiting for the others to arrive.

"Ah, Ms. Benson, you do not disappoint."

"I would be a fool to do so, Professor," she replied.

"And that you are not. We are going over chapter twenty, if you'd like to skim."

Lauren wasted no time turning to the chapter. She had only read up to chapter seventeen and knew she had some catching up to do.

"Hey, hey! Look who it is," Collin greeted, taking a seat beside her.

"Hey," she replied uncertainly.

"Glad you decided to come back. Where'd you move to?"

"I'm sorry, what?" she asked, confused.

"Tony and I stopped by your room, but you'd packed up and vanished."

"You stopped by to see me?"

He grinned wickedly. "Maybe."

Lauren couldn't make heads or tails of him. He leaned in, flipping the page of her book, pointing to a passage. "Art can be seen in the light of day, but the moon is the true visual to inspire artists to rise above the normal," she read aloud.

"In the moonlight, everything comes alive," he said. "I think that's my favorite line in the whole book."

Lauren stared into his green eyes, trying to find the real him inside. He'd never spoken anything as deep as that to her. Was he trying to impress her? He did think she was pretentious. She shook the thought of out her mind quickly.

"So," Collin inquired, "where'd you move to?"

The sound of a laugh rang out from her other side, and she was hardly shocked to find that it had come from Fallon.

"Off campus," Lauren replied, glaring at Fallon.

"Oh, don't be so secretive, Lauren. Just tell us..." Fallon goaded.

"I really need to catch up on the reading," Lauren said, ignoring both of them.

Collin sat back in his seat, rifling through his backpack for his book. Apparently, he wasn't going to be returning to his usual seat tonight. Lauren stifled a heavy sigh while trying to get back into her reading. She only made it halfway through the chapter before class began. She did her best to pay attention, although having Fallon openly watching her every move was unnerving.

"Who would like to start off class with a quick summary of the last chapter?" Professor asked. "Collin?"

Lauren watched how easily Collin slipped into the role of public speaker. There wasn't a trace of stress upon his smooth features as he adequately summarized the coursework. His eyes locked upon hers as he finished speaking, like his words were meant directly for her.

"Thank you, Collin. Anyone have anything to add?" Professor asked, looking around the room. "No? Okay, then let's get started..."

His voice began to drift out into the distance. Lauren stared at her book, trying to follow along. It felt as though a slow-moving fog had encompassed her mind. Her fingers gripped the sides of the book, forcing focus, although she had no clue where the class was.

"Page 243," Collin whispered. "Here..."

He leaned over, pointing to the section that was being discussed in her book. She glanced over at him in appreciation. The heat radiating from his side only produced more comfort, allowing him to turn the pages of her book that they were now reading together.

Her notebook was scribbled with notes and examples to remind her when she studied later on. Fallon tossed her book in her backpack as class was dismissed. Lauren packed up her bag following Collin into the aisle only to thumb towards the professor.

"I have to catch up on work," she advised.

"All right, see you later."

She went down the steps, taking a seat in the first row. Professor

Klein pulled out a small packet, handing it to her. She wasted no time, opening the packet and tugging out the midterm exam. The first page was multiple choice—easy enough for her to breeze through and into the next page, which was filled with short answer questions. She was elated seeing how easy it was and how much she was able to retain for it.

Lauren turned the page and stared blankly at the next page. The essay question section was next—long, drawn out questions with specific details requested. Her mind went completely blank as she read the first question twice over. She decided to skip the section to go back to later. The next part was matching the historical piece with the art fundamentals it represented. She pushed forward through the rest of the exam until only the essay questions were left.

The essay section was allotted the majority of the points for obvious reason. She closed her eyes, mentally trying to reread passages from the book that had any type of connection. She remembered something that resembled what the question was asking for, but couldn't be sure. She began writing to the best of her knowledge, which led her right into the next specific question. As she wrote, the answers came back, alive with fluid motion to detail certain aspects.

When she finished the exam, she double-checked it for anything missing before handing it back. She hadn't realized that while she was taking the exam, the professor had been going over notes for the next class.

"Thanks again," she said.

"No need to thank me, Ms. Benson. Those who want to learn find a way. I just leave the door open."

*****

Lauren had lain down in bed for merely a moment when her phone came to life. She quickly snatched it up and stared at Gina's name on the display. It was almost eleven o'clock at night and highly unusual for her to call this late.

"Hey, Gina," she greeted.

"Are you on campus?"

"Yeah, why?" she asked.

"Come to the room right away."

In the background, Lauren could hear crying and feared the worst. "I'm on my way."

Lauren jumped out of bed, throwing on her hoodie and jacket with a pair of jeans. She slid her feet into her pull-on boots as Taylor sat up in bed.

"I have to go out. Can I use your ID to get back in?"

"Yeah. You okay?" he asked, concerned.

"Yeah," she said, grabbing his ID from his desk and running out of the room.

The more she thought about the reasons why Hilary might be crying, the faster she pushed herself. It hadn't hit her until her feet were standing in front of her old room that she might have been blurring through campus. She knocked on the door out of respect for her old roommates, although she wanted to barge right in.

Gina opened the door, ushering her inside. Hilary was draped over her bed, her auburn hair splayed all over her pillow as she sobbed into the mattress. When Lauren glanced back at Gina, she had her hands shaped into two halves of a heart and then tilted them apart.

"Hilary?" Lauren whispered softly.

Her sobs quieted as she began to rub her face against the pillow.

"I'm going to need you to get dressed," Lauren said.

"Where are we going?" Gina asked.

"To the city," Lauren stated, laying her hands on the bed and bouncing Hilary on it. "Get dressed."

Hilary looked up with bloodshot eyes in disbelief. "No, I'm not going anywhere."

Lauren could see the hurt in her eyes as much as the anger towards her for moving out. Lauren turned to Gina and shrugged dramatically. "I guess I'm the fun roommate then. I'm spontaneous and adventurous. I certainly wouldn't regret my mistakes…"

"That's just stupid," Gina finished, staring back at Lauren. "I'm going to change my shirt."

Lauren watched Gina go to the dresser, hunting for the perfect top for the evening. Instead of trying to encourage Hilary to come along, Lauren went to the mirror and played with her hair. She even asked to borrow a nice top from Gina.

"I want to look my best for a night on the town…"

Slowly but surely, she noticed Hilary sit up on the bed, running her hands through her hair. Lauren kept from making eye contact as she threw out one last offer.

"I think an ice cream run would be perfect tonight."

"It's too cold for that," Gina complained.

"It's never too cold for ice cream," Hilary replied with a weak smile, wiping her nose. "Who's driving?"

Lauren smiled gently. "I am."

*****

The city was so bright, lit up by all the different establishments, billboards and streetlights. Cars were lined up down the side streets next to parking meters. To save on time, Lauren went to the parking garage, managing to snag a spot on the second floor. The girls piled out, leaving their coats and scarves, making a quick dash to the one place to cure any ailment.

Gina and Hilary went ahead into the building lit up with bright, multicolored neon lights. The stress lines that creased Hilary's forehead gently relaxed as she took in the atmosphere. The owner had taken creative liberty having the walls painted like the Caribbean beaches, setting the temperature higher than most places, with fans to push a light breeze. Even the tables had umbrellas fixed in the middle.

The girls went ahead, grabbing a table, while Lauren went to the bar, ordering jalapeño poppers, fries and three cokes. With her order number in hand, she sat at the table, leaving it displayed for the waiter. The sound of the gentle waves crashing into the surf played softly in the background allowing the patrons to completely ignore the fact that cold city life was bustling about on the sidewalk outside.

The waiter came over with the drinks first, placing them on the table.

"Can I get a Splash of Paradise?" Hilary asked, holding up her fake ID.

He checked the ID claiming her name was Patricia Pennington. She fluffed her hair and batted her eyes until a relaxed smile claimed his face.

"Sure thing."

Gina poked her roommate's side. "Don't get us kicked out. We've only just arrived."

"It'll be fine. I asked for a Splash, not whiskey on the rocks," Hilary replied, waving off Gina's worries. "Besides, after three years of a relationship going down the tubes, I think I deserve a drink."

Lauren had no reply, understanding how deep her pain must go. She certainly wasn't going to say anything about the drink knowing that she, too, had a fake ID in her wallet. It was a stupid decision she made in high school, but even now, she held onto it. She peered down at the ID that claimed her own name to be Francine Ferdinand.

"Don't worry, Gina. She wouldn't do anything to ruin the chances of us getting up there," Lauren stated, pointing to the corner covered in little lights with a microphone stand.

Gina's mouth dropped, not noticing the offending corner. "No."

Hilary's eyes lit up. "Really? You'd do that?"

"Tonight is all about you," Lauren replied. "Plus, we should practice for the talent show."

Hilary's eyes began to glisten as she nodded silently.

The requested Splash soon arrived, along with the appetizers. The jalapeño poppers were calling to Lauren. Not because she felt any need to eat, but because it was one of her favorite treats. She couldn't even remember the last time she ate, it had been so long.

She delicately picked one up within her fingers, blowing on the hot exterior. She opened her mouth and bit it in half, allowing the flavor to sink in. Every moment was the most pleasurable, painful and exciting. No matter how long she blew on it, the hot food burned her tongue, not just from the temperature but also because of the jalapeño.

"Are you all right?" Gina asked.

Lauren grabbed her coke, sipping it to quench the fire. "Mmmhhmmm..."

She sat back in her seat, feeling the contents lower into her stomach. If there was a cartoon reenactment, her mouth would have breathed fire, needing an extinguisher to drench her completely. And when the popper hit her stomach, it would have made a *pang* type of noise.

Gina steered clear of the spicy appetizer, munching on fries, while Hilary sucked down her drink. When she finished, she left the table only to come back with the karaoke playlist.

Gina groaned, "Are you sure you don't want another drink?"

Hilary poked her in the arm. "Yes, I'd love one. After we sing."

Gina groaned even more dramatically towards Lauren. "This is your fault."

"This one! I wanna sing this one!" Hilary exclaimed.

Lauren glanced at the selection and held back her own groan. It was Girl Power by The Termites. Hilary knew every word and could keep a tune without issue. Gina, on the other hand, was a fabulous singer. Lauren had caught her a couple of times in the room but never mentioned it, noticing how self-conscious she was about it. Apparently, neither one of the roommates had ever heard a peep out of Lauren. She wasn't able to carry a tune, clearly the reason why she'd joined the high school band instead.

Hilary ushered the three of them over to the karaoke machine, talking to the bartender about which selection they'd like to sing. They got in place at the microphone in the corner with the dangling lights as the music began to play. Hilary and Gina were side-by-side at the microphone while Lauren held back. As the song began, their voices intertwined, calling to every woman to stand up for her right to be all she is.

From where Lauren stood, she could tell Gina was nervous, but singing the best she could in a serious way. Hilary, on the other hand, was singing freely, arms extended into the air, hips rocking from side to side, just enjoying the moment for what it was. Lauren practically whispered the lyrics until the song ended, and Hilary was jumping up and down out of excitement.

"That was awesome!" Hilary exclaimed as they reached their table.

Gina agreed, sipping her drink, the goosebumps clearly visible on her arms.

"Time for ice cream?" Lauren asked.

"Yes! Although, I didn't hear *you* singing very loudly," Hilary complained.

"It's not one of my strong points."

Lauren flagged down the waiter, asking for ice creams for the table. He left just as quickly allowing the resonating glow of the performance to linger a while longer.

*****

The night air was crisp as she left her old dorm, heading towards Taylor's room. It was easily past midnight now, but the campus seemed to come alive. The moonlight shone down in beautiful rays, lighting the pathway. She thought of what Collin had said earlier that day. Indeed, only true artists can find the beauty in the night.

"You know, it's never a good idea to walk alone at night."

Lauren took in the sight of a dark shadow walking towards her. Her alarm bells weren't going off, though, but seemed to laugh aloud. "I was just thinking about what you said. Finding beauty at night."

Collin strolled over to her side. "It's pretty accurate in my opinion. May I ask what you're doing out this late?"

"Had a girl's night out. It was well overdue," she replied. "And you?"

"Watched a basketball game that went into overtime."

She remained silent, already picturing Tony spending time occupied with entertainment and friends to get over the breakup. It was exactly what she'd done with Hilary, albeit a bit more fun on her end.

As they passed by the trees that had once caused anxiety, she seemed to resonate with who she'd become over the past month. She knew herself well enough to know that walking around with an acquaintance this late at night wouldn't have happened before. The mere fact that she wasn't as tucked within herself spoke volumes.

The dorm soon appeared, bathed in the moonlight like it was welcoming her home. She thought of Taylor sleeping quietly in the room and how she'd have to quietly get inside. Her chest and throat warmed unusually as she grazed her fingers across the skin of her neck nervously.

"Do you have plans for tomorrow?" Collin asked.

She shook off the feeling, trying to think about his question. "I don't believe so. Why?"

"You're really going to make me work for this, aren't you?" He took two long strides, turning to face her full on, causing her to stop. He reached out only to take hold of her hands securely. "Go out with me."

Lauren couldn't believe her ears. He had asked her out… or well, told her to. She stared up at him, trying to form a response. Admitting any interest in dating him was pointless. He couldn't handle what she was… not that she could, either. She wouldn't want to lie to him, and if he got closer to her, that would surely happen.

"Well?" he asked, searching her eyes, only just becoming slowly aware that she hadn't jumped at the opportunity.

"I'm sorry," she began to say as her stomach began to protest strongly to the contents within it. "I've got to go."

Lauren pulled her hands from him, making a full sprint into the building. Once inside, she blurred up the stairs and into the restroom. She just made it into the stall as her earlier treats made a reappearance. Her legs wobbled as she went to the sink and began to rinse out her mouth, doing her best to ignore the black sludge that swirled down the drain.

She leaned heavily against the walls of the hallway, taking her time going into her room. Toeing off her boots as she sat on the bed while pulling her hoodie off over her head was a feat in itself. All she wanted to do was curl up in a ball and be left alone. Unfortunately, she knew that the alarm would be going off soon enough for her morning class.

Not bothering to change since moving was making her feel worse, she lay back on the top of her bed and allowed her body to rest.

Chapter Thirteen

"Lauren, wake up," Taylor's voice said as he shook her shoulder. "Get up."

When she opened her eyes, there was no sign of ill effects from the night before. She rolled over slowly, allowing her sock-covered feet to rest on the floor. Still there was no protest from her stomach, which left hope for her getting through her only class of the day.

Grabbing her hoodie and spraying body fragrance would suffice for an eight a.m. course. She grabbed her backpack and slid her feet into her shoes as she felt eyes on her again. She didn't have time, nor did she want to explain what had happened previously. She left the room in silence, not acknowledging her best friend.

*****

The music was blasting when she approached the dorm room. She didn't have to guess which band or song was playing as she could hear that clearly through the door. She checked the doorknob for any sign of "Keep Out," but there was nothing. She cautiously went inside only to find Taylor actually making his bed with the windows open about an inch to allow a breeze.

Maybe she'd just missed his company? She did her best to try to ignore the idea. She closed the door behind her, not that he could hear her come in. She went to her side of the room, tossing her backpack on the floor beside the bed and removing her hoodie and shoes for comfort. Noticing her return, he turned the music down considerably.

"You left your phone," he casually mentioned. "I think you've got some text messages."

Lauren looked at the offending electronic device sitting on the dresser. She was curious and fearful all at once. She had essentially blown off Collin, one of the hottest guys on campus. Was he calling her out on it? She already began shaking her head and backing up towards her bed. "Why do I feel like you've already checked my messages?"

Taylor laughed. "Because you know me."

She continued to sit down on the bed and lie back to stare at the ceiling. "Is it bad?"

"I didn't read them… fully. Hilary goes on and on. I guess she and Tony are talking things through tonight," he said.

"Oh. Good. I'm glad."

He went over to his desk, tapping on his laptop. "So Collin, huh?"

Her body stilled on the bed. So he *had* texted her. How was it that when she had her phone with her, no one ever reached out, but when she wasn't near it, it blew up? What had he said? Was he pissed?

"I don't want to know, Taylor. Not now."

He shrugged from his seat. "You only have so long to give him an answer."

That sat her up. "Answer what?"

Taylor turned to face her. "You have plans with him, clearly. He wanted to confirm a time."

Her rapid movement sent an unpleasant lurch through her stomach. There wasn't even a protest to alert her, only the warm liquid filling her mouth. She grabbed the closest bin, getting sick into it. She felt a warm hand upon her back while another pulled her hair out of the way.

Lauren sat back, feeling beyond exhausted and gross.

"I wouldn't have mentioned it if it was going to make you sick."

"It's me. Not you."

"What do you mean? Are you sick?" he asked.

"Call Quinn."

Taylor grabbed her phone, bringing it to her. She waiting as the phone rang over and over. The sound of Quinn's voice over the voicemail wasn't what she wanted to hear. Her fingers tugged a few tissues from the Kleenex box, swiping at her mouth after spitting a few times.

Links & Chains began to play from her phone, and she answered without looking. "Quinn?"

"What's going on, Lauren?"

"I ate," she said, trying not to get sick again. "So stupid."

"What? What did you do?" His voice came across acidic.

"Coke, jalapeño poppers." She wanted to vomit again just saying out aloud. "Ice cream."

"Lauren…" He stopped talking as a ruffled noise sounded. "Are you suicidal?"

"What? No. Of course not."

"Are you delusional?"

"No," she seethed.

"Then why are you trying to eat human foods? You're not—I repeat, not—human!"

She opened her mouth to respond as the urge came back. She

dropped the phone beside her as she hurled into the basket again. Taylor picked up the phone and stepped back towards the window.

"She needs a minute," Taylor said into the line, putting it on speaker.

"Why would she do such a stupid thing? She's putting her life in danger." Quinn huffed a few times before more ruffled noises sounded over the phone. "How long has she been doing this?"

"Eating?"

"Vomiting," Quinn clarified.

"This morning—" Taylor began to say when Lauren interrupted with a shake of her head. "Last night."

"Shit. Bring her to the lab. As fast as you can."

"What's wrong with me?" she asked.

"Food poisoning, essentially. And it's lethal."

The phone went silent and then dead. His words hung heavily in the air. *Lethal.* She looked up at her best friend. Her words were lost, and the ability to move seemed impossible. Taylor slid her phone into his pocket.

"Let's go," he said calmly. Too calmly.

Her legs protested along with her mouth. She placed her hands firmly on the ground, trying to raise up. Her efforts were less than desired as she tried with wobbly legs to stand up fully. Her energy level had dipped so low that she ended up sitting back on the bed.

"I-I can't," she huffed.

He reached out to help her up just as another round of sickness made her stick her head back into the wastebasket. He took out her phone, dialing on speakerphone. He didn't wait for a response. "She's not going anywhere. What can I do to help her?"

"Am I on speaker phone?" Quinn asked.

"Yes."

"Lauren, listen to me. I'm going to have Taylor do what I need to get you better, all right? So you need to do everything he says. Everything."

She couldn't respond, busily getting sick.

"She'll do it," Taylor responded.

"Take me off speaker."

Her eyes lifted at that request, not trusting it at all. Taylor turned his back on her as he picked up a pen from his desk, taking down notes. He seemed to nod along until the pen stopped on the paper. "You're crazy. She won't do it."

His stance became tense all at once. He listened intently as his grip became fatal for the pen within it, snapping it in two pieces and sending ink all over his hand. He tossed the pen in his wastebasket and grabbed a tissue to try to wipe it off.

He left the phone between his ear and shoulder. "Be right back," he said to Lauren, gesturing to go wash his hand.

Carefully lying back on the bed, she stared at the ceiling. Her throat ached as her eyes began to close. She was so tired that taking a nap felt like a good idea. Her mind was easily cleared of worries and concerns as she took note of relaxing her muscles and joints.

A warm hand brushed against her jaw. Her eyes refused to open as something soft and warm pressed to her lips. She didn't want to eat anything after feeling like the biggest idiot. Still, the pressure increased as she used her hands to try to push back.

"Relax, just drink," Taylor stated.

His request was strange as she wasn't noticing anything even happening. She brushed her lips against the warm substance until she realized what it was. Even then her eyes stayed practically glued shut. She panicked, twisting her head from side to side to get away. A strong grip on her jaw painfully halted the movement, as the pressure against her lips increased.

"Stop fighting me," Taylor complained in a strained voice. "I'm trying to help."

"No!" she yelled before clamping down on his finger.

"Fuck!" Taylor shouted before she opened her mouth, releasing him.

She tried to spit out as much as possible but the salty taste wouldn't leave her tongue. Her throat clogged up with emotion as she curled up in a ball. It struck her then how intensely upset she was. There was nothing she could do about it. She wasn't human anymore. No more spoonsful of her favorite dessert would ever come again. It could have ended her.

After a minute, her eyes blinked open without issue. Her stomach had settled down quietly, not rolling anymore, even though she had turned over. Her eyes sprang open directly at Taylor. He was busy holding his hand and swearing in the background. As much as she wanted to yell at him, she couldn't. She had put herself in this position.

"I didn't mean to bite you," she said. He ignored her, trying to focus on his wound. She went over, reaching for his hand. "Let me see..."

Taylor turned his back on her, which she could guess was out of anger. She sighed heavily, grabbing his bicep and forcefully twisting him back. She wasted no time gripping his wrist, tugging the hand towards her. It wasn't bleeding hardly at all, but the tiny rows of teeth marks caused distress.

"I'm sorry. It'll fade," she responded, trying to gently massage the marks away with her fingertips. Her lips trembled as emotion began to rumble within her chest. This was what Quinn had been worried about from the beginning. Her being a danger to innocent people. Granted, this was extremely small scale, but still not for her.

Taylor withdrew his hand as she panicked within. "Do you feel better now?"

No. She felt so much worse. Not wanting to voice it aloud, she nodded for his benefit. She went back to her bed with the wastebasket filled with her life source. She gripped her fists wanting to scream.

"I have to get to class. Are you sure you're okay?" His voice was stern and cold, merely checking on her out of habit.

She nodded again until she heard the door close behind him. She took two deep breaths to calm herself although it seemed to only send more frantic energy through her. She bit him. Her best friend. She drank his blood... like a monster.

The painful thought was ricocheting through her mind. The memory of the warm substance touching her tongue, gliding across the surface and down her throat. The savory taste still echoed within her mouth, which was begging for more. She fell to her knees clutching her arms around herself.

She was near sobbing on the inside. It struck her then that she couldn't cry. Her thoughts flew back to Quinn and his example with the yellow-tainted water. There was no water left within her. Her life force had changed.

Lauren noticed her phone sitting on Taylor's desk. She went to it, dialing the one person who could answer her questions. The phone rang a few times before it picked up.

"Taylor?"

"No," she responded.

"Ah, so you're feeling better."

"What. The. Hell." She couldn't manage more than that.

"Shouldn't I be saying that to you? Don't be hard on him. You put him in that position," Quinn said. "You wouldn't have made it, you know."

"Wasn't that your plan anyway? Get all the answers and research you can before having me put down by your girlfriend?"

"Lauren—"

"Was that another test? See how many times I can take a deep knifing before I die? Did I pass?" Her words angrily flew out through gritted teeth.

"Fallon stabbed you?"

"Don't play dumb with me. How else could she have hidden her bruises from the toss I gave her," she said.

"I had no idea it was from you... but I should have."

"So tell me this, how much of this black stuff do I need to lose before dying?" Lauren asked.

"Normal Bellators don't have to worry about it. They are constantly feeding, and it replenishes. You're different in more ways than one, Lauren."

"I'm dangerous..."

"Of course you are; however, it's more complex than I first thought. I have never seen DNA like yours. Dare I say you're an oxymoron," he quipped. "I want to show you what I mean."

Lauren didn't want to go anywhere near him. Thoughts of being near anyone was insane. She went to the side of the bed, picking up the lantern to inspect it further. How was this supposed to make her want to join the side of the Bellators? She certainly didn't want anything to do with them, but she obviously couldn't be living this close to humans.

"I've tested more than several Bellators, Lauren. While every one of them had a slight difference within, there was a sequence that every single one of them had. I thought it was part of what made them who they were. You just blew that theory away."

She put the phone on speaker and set it on the dresser. She pulled out her bag, grabbing handfuls of clothes to shove inside. Only when the bag was filled did she turn back to the lantern. Would she take it with her? Should she?

"When can you get here?" Quinn asked.

"I'm not."

"This is a huge deal, Lauren. Do you know what this could mean?" he asked intently. "Your DNA could be the cure..."

Her hand gripped the handle of the bag, lifting it from the bed. "Yeah, right. You couldn't possibly know that."

"You haven't been around lately to see what I have already done. Come here and check for yourself."

"Fine. See you in ten," she conceded.

The condemned building appeared to find new life covered in the frost of winter. She imagined nature taking a delicate brush to the outer exterior, coating it with the shimmering ice, covering up the eyesore it had become. The interior wasn't coated entirely, thanks to some of the boards holding from the second floor. The few tables and chairs scattered about glistened in the sunlight.

She descended the stairs to the basement, going inside the lab. Quinn was grabbing syringes from the closet and placing them in upright holders. She noticed the cage where the small white mouse had been kept, although it was empty now. Quinn continued grabbing a few items before acknowledging her.

"How are you feeling?"

"I'm not throwing up anymore," she replied.

"Clearly," he said, unamused. "How many drops did he give you?"

"Drops?"

"Of blood..." he pushed.

"I don't know. I wasn't really in a mental place to be counting them."

"Sit," he ordered.

Lauren rolled her eyes as she went over to the lab table. He took out a pair of gloves and an alcohol swab. She knew what he wanted to check, and why, but it made her nervous. What if he would find out how dangerous she was now?

"Is this really necessary? I thought you were going to show me something."

"Yes, I am, but fresh contents would be more accurate. Are you opposed?" he questioned, scrutinizing her with his eyes.

"I've already lost so much..." She paused a moment and then continued, "How long does it take to replenish?"

"What's wrong with you?"

"Nothing," she replied.

"Are you hungry now?"

"It's pretty stupid of you to ask me now. Hate to burst your bubble, but no, I'm not." Lauren said, irritated. "I don't really have time for this. Can you hurry up?"

Quinn gave her a hard once over as he reached out a hand for her arm. "As soon as you oblige me with a sample."

Reluctantly, she didn't resist his request seeing that he wasn't going to move forward without it. She could only hope that the recent feeding would have little change or effect on what he saw. Her breaths became shallow as he pricked her skin and slid the needle into the vein, slowly taking some of her life force. This time, he only took one tube's worth; she wondered if he was concerned about how much she'd lost already.

Quinn went to work, using two petri dishes to contain a few drops. His skillful hands grabbed a few different bottles placing a drop of each in the dish. He took it over to the microscope, focused. She fidgeted on the stool wishing to be in the loaded car already.

"Hmmm..." he said while twisting the knobs. "Interesting."

Lauren glanced down at her cell phone. She was losing more

time than she had planned. "I have to go, Quinn."

He glanced up at her in confusion, like within the few minutes, he'd forgotten she was still sitting there. "Sorry. Come look at this."

The empty cage on the table was soon filled by one small gray mouse. "What happened to the white one? Where's this one come from?"

"It's the same mouse," Quinn said as he checked the small bowl of food inside. "I injected him with a small amount of your DNA, and this is what happened."

The gray mouse carefully checked its surroundings. His tiny eyes scanned the food bowl before dismissing it completely. He looked at the water dropper for a mere moment before turning his back on that, as well. When he looked up noticing Quinn, the tiny hairs on his back raised up slightly, backing farther away until he was pressed against the side of the cage.

"Since the injection, he has been without appetite or thirst. And the sight of me scares the crap out of him."

"Why didn't I see him before?" she asked.

"He hides. It's not because of the bright lights because I cover him up. He chooses to hide."

She leaned down to get a closer look as the mouse turned its eyes on her. The tiny mouse seemed to panic before squeaking over and over. Her brow creased with concern. "What's wrong, little one?"

"Can you understand him?" Quinn asked dubiously.

"It doesn't take a rocket scientist to see that he doesn't like it in here," she said, looking at the cage. "He wants to be free."

"That's interesting. He hates me clearly and doesn't care for

162

Fallon, either. Yet, here he is looking at you for help. Maybe a blood connection..."

She wondered if her emotions were wrapped up within her blood. Part of her wanted to take him with her. Break him out of his mousey jail so that he could be happy elsewhere, but would he fit in now? He was changed just like she was. Were they allowed to be part of the world?

Her fingers instinctively went to the latch to undo it. The mouse willingly crawled towards her hand as she carefully scooped him up. His fur was soft as he sat still although she could feel his panic. She lightly pet him until he calmed.

"He's not a pet, Lauren."

"No, he's not a pet. Just a living creature wanting to do just that," she replied. "Do you think he'd find love out there? Create a family of his own?"

"As long as there's no males around to challenge him, maybe." Quinn went back to the microscope to check the second dish. "Make sure you put him back, though. He isn't prepared for life outside of that cage. Especially in his condition."

Her heart ached as she watched him crawl up her arm and sit upon her shoulder. She knew that if she'd allowed it, Quinn would have locked her away, too. She would have been miserable and hated him.

"Have you offered him human blood?"

Quinn laughed. "He doesn't take a step near it when I do."

She pet him gently on her shoulder, and he squeaked a pleasant sound. She could get used to this too easily. A quick glance at the clock on her phone set her pulse into a frenzy. She'd spent way too long here now. She lifted the mouse from her shoulder and held it at eye level. Could she leave him behind? His tiny nose grazed her fingers and knew the answer.

"Quinn, I'm going to head out for a while. Can I take him with me?"

"No, put him back," he said.

"I promise to keep him safe. I just can't bear to leave him yet," she replied as the mouse grasped the edges of her fingers and bumped its nose to hers. "Please?"

Quinn only shook his head in disagreement. "He's in transition, Lauren. The eclipse won't be for another six months. He needs as much stability as possible. I'm sorry, but the answer is no. Now put him back."

Reluctantly, she carried him back to the cage door opening. Seeing his destination, he protested and squirmed in the cutest way. She held him carefully until his paws touched the floor of the cage. His tiny eyes glared at her in frustration.

"Shhh…" she whispered to the tiny creature. "Let me know of any new developments," she said to Quinn as she made her way to the door.

He nodded a farewell to her as he kept working with the new sample. As she left the building, her mind scrambled for an explanation to give when Taylor called. And he would. She got into her vehicle and sat with her things surrounding her. There was only one place she could go. She started the car and went home.

Chapter Fourteen

The house was quiet as she entered as her lone car sat in the driveway. She hadn't told her parents that she'd be coming home, not that it mattered to her. She wasn't in the mood to shop around with her mom. She took her bags to her room, dropping them on the floor before sitting down on her bed.

Her phone had stayed silent thanks to the use of the power button. The more she thought about it, the tighter her stomach knotted. She wasn't sure who she feared hearing from more, Taylor or Collin. Not wanting to think of either, she went over to her music stand. Sheets awaited her attention, the exact distraction she needed to feel like her old self.

Her fingers floated over the flute like she'd never stopped playing. She kept tempo with her foot as the serene energy cloaked her. This was her special place, where she could blossom within herself. While she had enjoyed band in school, it was a particular favorite to enjoy it alone.

An hour had easily passed until a knock on the door sought her attention. Her mom smiled as she leaned against the doorframe. "It's nice to have music back in this house."

"Thanks."

"May I ask why the sudden stop home? Laundry already out?"

"There was nowhere else I wanted to be," she said, disassembling her instrument.

"Oh, no, don't stop on my account. I'm going to order a pizza, okay?"

Lauren nodded, holding her grimace inside. She would have to figure a way around that. Her mom had quietly walked back down the hall. She replaced her flute back in its case and moved the stand back into the corner.

Her cell phone was burning a hole in her pocket. Her curiosity aside, now that she was feeling calmer, she could handle her human responsibilities. She turned on the device and waited for the messages that she hoped wouldn't come. As the text notifications began to sound off, she sat on the bed, trying to keep her serenity.

She tackled the first few from Hilary—she and Tony were indeed talking but not back together. That was a surprise coming from Hilary. For someone so into pushing others into relationships, she wasn't jumping back into her own. The details weren't given as to why they'd broken up to begin with, but it was a moot point now.

Collin had sent three text messages hours apart, checking on the time for tonight. She clearly wasn't going to be attending. How was she supposed to have a normal relationship with him? If that was what he was asking for. She was starting to feel more and more like her mousy friend. She might not be in a cage, but she certainly wasn't free either.

Her favorite song bellowed at her, erasing all concern over Collin. Taylor's name flashed across the screen, and no matter how much she wanted to ignore it, she answered. She had some explaining to do or maybe more apologizing? She couldn't be sure which mood he'd be in now.

"Hi..."

"Are you coming back tonight?" he asked.

"I don't think so."

"All right. Well, have fun on your date," he said.

166

"There is no date."

"Collin blew you off?" Taylor asked.

"He has no idea what he's getting into being around me. It would be impossible to date him. It's not fair to him."

"We are talking about the same guy, right? 'Dating' isn't what he's known for," he stated.

"Yeah, and that can mean only two things. He either is interested in doing one thing, which isn't even a possibility, or he's turned over a new leaf. I'm highly doubtful of the latter."

"I'm not disagreeing with you. So then, what are you doing tonight?"

"My bed looks like the main event. I'll be sure to get back before class starts on Monday," she replied.

"You went home? Are you shitting me?"

"I figured you wouldn't want to be around me," she explained.

"Obviously, I wasn't happy you bit me, but I wasn't going to kick you out over it. Why would you think to go all the way home instead of at least talking to me first?"

Her frustration slowly built until she finally spat out what had had her worried all along. "I don't want to hurt you, Taylor. I've never consumed blood before and..." She took a second to find the right wording. "It tasted... good. I'm not thirsty or having any cravings, but that scared the life out of me."

Silence befell the line, although she could hear his breathing. Quietly, he asked, "Do you want more?"

"I'm not feeding off of you."

"That's not what I asked, Lauren. Do you?"

"I've had a long day already between getting sick and officially canceling any chance of having a happy future. I'm calling it a day," she said, hanging up.

Lauren took the stairs down to the living room and got comfortable on the couch, only to hear her dad coming in from the front door. He headed for the TV, although he took it in stride to find her sitting there already. He grabbed the remote control and put on the football game.

"Hey, kiddo, didn't know you were coming down this weekend."

"Things are a bit tense up at the college. Who's playing tonight?" she asked.

"Washington and Colorado. Where's your mother?"

"Picking up pizza, I think," she replied, stretching her legs out. "What's new with you, Dad?"

"Eh, same old, same old. Working, sleeping and football."

Lauren laughed. "Clearly, I made the right choice."

They settled into their seats, completely at ease watching the teams battle for the win. Her mom knew not to bother them other than to place the pizza box on the coffee table and bring in cups with a bottle of soda. Lauren still hadn't figured out a way to get around eating, but with the touchdowns becoming more inconsistent, the distraction was easy.

Her father's hands gripped the arms of the chair as he leaned forward staring at the screen. The soft blue surrounding his irises was dominated by the reflection from the game. As she took in her father, she once again wished to be more like him.

She'd always admired his easy-going mentality, not bothered by any of the excessive requests made by her mom, including the last minute, late night errands he'd be dragged along for. She could tell by the neutral expression he gave when asked that he would rather be doing anything else, but his willingness to support them was one thing she loved the most.

When the team retreated for halftime, Lauren began to clean up the pizza box and cups. She wrapped up the leftover slices and placed them in the fridge as her phone sang in her pocket. The display showed it was Taylor calling, and she was unsure of what to do. She answered, although part of her wanted to chuck the device in the trash.

"Hey—"

"I need your help," he stated seriously.

Lauren could hear the panic in his voice although he tried to mask it. "Okay?"

"Marcus is in the county jail."

"What?!"

"Dad is out of town. He's all alone," he said.

"Taylor—"

"I'm on my way to the jail and should be there within fifteen minutes. Please, Lauren," he asked.

"Okay."

"Thanks," he said before hanging up.

Lauren went up to her room to grab her jacket and scarf before descending the stairs. She went into the den where her mom sat, reading a book with headphones on. Clearly, her mom wasn't exaggerating about how loud Dad could be. Her mom looked up as she walked closer.

"You're going out?"

"I have to go see a friend," she said.

"All right. Be safe and make sure to wear your seatbelt. They're cracking down hard now."

Lauren nodded. "Will do."

"Is Taylor back?"

"What? Why would you ask that?" she questioned.

"He's the only person I've ever seen you take off this quickly for," her mom said with a gentle smile.

"Ummm... yeah. I won't be out too late."

Her mom went over, placing a comforting hand on her shoulder. "Finally, huh?"

Lauren's eyebrows scrunched together. "What?"

"You and Taylor?"

"Oh, Mom, stop. We're friends. *Best* friends," she said.

"The best relationships sprout from that very thing. Your father and I were college sweethearts and—"

"Fell madly in love and married after getting your degrees. I know, I know, but that's your life, not mine. Taylor and I... we're not like that."

"Honey, I'm not trying to pressure you. Life offers many veiled possibilities. Taylor is a good boy; his father has done an amazing job raising both of those boys by himself. Just don't be so quick to write him off."

Lauren nodded to placate her. Her mind might change should

she know where Marcus was sitting at the moment. Thoughts of being anything more with Taylor was always forbidden. He wouldn't even try dating for any female; she wasn't any exception. Her best friend status was her saving grace.

Lauren hugged her mom before leaving into the cold evening air. She got into the car and drove down the street. The houses were all different variations of two story homes in pastel colors. Trees lined the street as the leaves twitched in the gentle breeze. She'd forgotten how quiet it could be at night during the school year.

As she drove closer to the town center, the lampposts became more vivid and brighter. It only took a few turns to reach the county jail. She'd taken a tour of the jail as a child, and after seeing how uncomfortable and smelly it was, vowed to stay on the right side of the law.

Her hands pulled open the door as she went inside and approached the front desk. A young officer sat focused on the papers littering his desk. She waited patiently for him to notice her. Unfortunately, he wasn't in the mood to deal with her for more than a few seconds.

"Can I help you?" he asked, still mulling over the papers.

"My friend was brought in tonight. I was wondering if—"

"No one can visit except family and an attorney," he said, cutting her off.

"I understand. Can you at least tell him—"

"Listen, there's nothing I can do for you. You might as well go home and get some sleep."

There was no way she could just leave. And with the officer

being uncooperative, she could only stay silent. She took a seat in the lobby waiting for Taylor to arrive. She shook her head in disappointment at the turn of events. Even now, she could remember how it all began…

It had been a month of muted friendship when Taylor's little brother, Marcus, met them at the corner of her street.

"Taylor! I found this awesome tree to climb. It's so tall," Marcus said excitedly. "Hi, Lauren."

"Hey, Marcus," she said cautiously, noting how Taylor hadn't responded at all. "Where's this tree?"

"It's at the park but pushed farther back."

"Isn't that trespassing on Old Tavares' property?" she asked.

Marcus shrugged. "I've climbed it without getting caught."

Lauren turned to Taylor with worry. She didn't want to get into trouble, and this was definitely going to be. Taylor's expression transformed from stone silence to a menacing grin. He nodded towards Marcus in acceptance.

She watched them start to take off without her. She knew better than to trespass on others' property. It would be stupid to get caught, and her parents would be so upset with her. Although, Marcus had done it already and not gotten caught. And if Taylor was there, maybe they really could get away with it.

Before she realized it, her feet were already treading speedily on the pavement towards them. Marcus seemed thrilled with her attempt to follow and ran across the street towards the park. Taylor followed suit, bypassing even his little brother with his speed, easily taking the lead.

Running wasn't one of her talents, but she did what she could to keep up with them. It didn't change the fact that she was the last to arrive at the park. She noticed Taylor walking towards the edge of the park first and quickly made it over to his side. He stared ahead, in between the trees and shadows, until something caught his attention.

"You don't have to come," Taylor said, not looking at her.

"I know."

"Then why are you?" he asked.

"It sounded like fun. Do you want me to leave?"

"I don't care," he said, pushing forward.

She watched his back as the light dimmed through the shadows of the trees. She knew how mean he could be; she'd seen it before with others. This wasn't that bad in the scheme of things. Knowing that he hadn't really been himself for a while only encouraged her to continue.

Marcus stood at the bottom of the tree proudly. She looked up the tall trunk in awe. She'd never seen one so tall in her life. The branches were thinner than others she'd seen and with little foliage near the bottom. It certainly looked like an interesting climb from where she stood.

"How high did you go?"

"Pretty high, but then I saw his truck pull into the driveway. Didn't want to get caught so I came down," Marcus explained.

The trio looked towards the driveway, finding it empty. Marcus smirked, grabbing a branch and lifting himself up. Taylor wasted no time doing the same. Lauren glanced back at the driveway as the fear of getting caught really started to sink in. Would she go up the tree, too?

The brothers didn't seem to notice her lack of accompaniment. They chose different routes towards the top that fit their personality. Marcus grabbed any branch within reach to pull himself up, while Taylor selected only certain branches and ascended faster than Marcus.

173

A low buzzing began to sound on the ground close to a few bushes. The sound was slowly changing tempo from a consistent chorus to a vibrant climax. Lauren glanced up her friends, but they were too high to notice. Her eyes scanned the bushes until she noticed the one on the end that was stirring from the vibration. When she stared harder, she noticed that almost every inch of it was moving.

Fear paralyzed her as the buzzing fluctuated until a few small insects broke away from the interior of the bush. They began to circle the bush with more joining in. Within seconds, a huge swarm danced merely a few feet from where she stood.

"You coming?" Marcus shouted from above.

Lauren couldn't tear her eyes away from the swarm. As more insects joined in, the further it spread out, getting ever closer. She wasn't sure if running was even an option or if she just stayed put, maybe they'd not notice her standing there.

"Lauren?" Marcus asked, leaning in her direction, stepping on a small branch. It cracked beneath his weight, breaking off and tumbling down the tree. He clung to the tree, quickly finding placement for his feet as the branch bounced off of the bark, ricocheting right at the bees, causing them to buzz frantically within the swarm.

Panic engulfed her as they began to zip around, headed straight for her. She screamed aloud, finally finding her feet and running towards the park. The buzzing became louder until sharp needle-like stingers broke through her skin. She swatted at them to keep them away, but her vision was slowly beginning to darken. The park appeared so far away as her legs gave out, sending her to the ground.

The surroundings were growing hazy and dark as her eyes slowly began to close.

"I got here as quickly as I could. How's he doing?" Taylor asked quickly.

"He doesn't know I'm here. They wouldn't tell him."

Taylor went straight to the officer sitting at the desk. "Marcus Kelley."

"What about him?"

"He's my brother. Can I see him?" Taylor stated.

"ID?" the officer requested. He checked the verification and pulled out a clipboard for him to sign. "You can come see him for a minute. Just you."

Taylor glanced towards Lauren, and she nodded understanding.

"What are you holding him for?"

"Disorderly conduct, disturbing the peace and fighting in a public restaurant," the officer stated.

Chapter Fifteen

Lauren checked the circular clock hanging in the lobby just as Taylor emerged from the back. His face was distorted with anger as he pushed the doors open, going outside. She followed him as he unlocked his car.

"Taylor?"

"He's not going anywhere until Monday. Dad will be back by then," he said, pulling open the car door.

"Had he been drinking?"

"Marcus is as sober as we are. Doesn't change the fact that he's irrational and refuses to take responsibility for his actions." He climbed inside the vehicle, starting it, and drove off.

Lauren watched the tail lights of his black car disappear around the corner. She knew he was upset about Marcus and shouldn't take offense at his attitude or actions, but she couldn't help it. She'd come home wanting to relax and spend time with her family, not to be dragged into his family drama.

She climbed behind the wheel of her own vehicle with an irritated sigh. Marcus couldn't help but get into trouble; it was almost as if he enjoyed the displeasure it gave his family. She could only imagine the trouble he'd get into if he'd spent a weekend at school with them. He'd cause havoc within a few hours knowing that he could just leave. Taylor would be left with the after-effects, not that Marcus cared.

Lauren drove home, trying to find the peace she'd had before Taylor had called. Nostalgia was always a good choice in her opinion. Maybe a night of childhood movies could salvage the night. As she turned into her street, she was mystified to find Taylor's car idling in front of her house.

She parked in the driveway, watching the passenger side window roll down as she approached. Taylor stared ahead merely sensing her presence. "Get in."

"I don't feel like going out tonight."

"Good," he continued.

Lauren rolled her eyes and pointed to her house. "Mom is waiting for me."

"Tell her you're coming to hang with me. She wouldn't mind, and we both know it."

"She already knows I went to see you tonight."

Taylor pushed the car door open. "Then she doesn't need to know anything else. Come on."

Against her better judgment, she climbed into the passenger seat. She hadn't fully recovered from her earlier irritation, and his attitude wasn't helping matters. She closed the car door, and he pulled away from the curb.

"I'm not even supposed to be here," he mumbled under his breath.

Technically, she wasn't supposed to be there, either. Her evening had changed quite a bit from the quiet plans she'd originally contemplated. As he turned the corner towards his dark, empty home, she questioned why she'd gotten in the car with him at all.

Taylor parked in the long, slender driveway. He pulled out his keys as he went to the side entrance, and she followed him down the stairs into the basement level room he'd created for himself. He flicked on the light switch and tossed his keys on the end table before collapsing on the couch and turning on the TV.

"Aren't you going to call your dad?" she asked, still standing at the door.

"I will, eventually."

"Taylor, think of your brother—"

"I am. He's in the one place where he can be held accountable," he interrupted angrily.

"What would your dad say?"

Taylor glared at her. "I'm doing Marcus a favor. Dad has always been soft on him, and look where he is now? Dad can enjoy at least one night away from home. So, you see, I'm thinking of everyone, unlike my brother."

Lauren could feel the warmth pooling in her chest as her irritation rose. "You thought of everyone?"

"Why are you trying to fight with me on this? I didn't invite you over to argue."

"You didn't invite me over. You commanded it. Just like you needed me to stop what I was doing to come help you tonight with Marcus. Heaven forbid you bother your dad about his son, but it's perfectly acceptable to just demand these things from me!"

"What the hell—"

"I'm the last person on your radar! You thought of everyone *but me*. And that's the point," she said, finally catching a breath. "I've finally got the point."

She grabbed the door, shoving it open as she strode up the stairs. Even the night air couldn't calm the tension within her shoulders. It only took her reaching the end of the driveway to regret her words.

Not that what she'd said wasn't true; but he'd had other worries on his mind, least of all her. She shouldn't have said anything. She should have stayed home.

"Lauren."

Her back stiffened at the sound of his voice. He'd followed her, probably to get a word in since she'd practically yelled his house down and left. Part of her wanted to take back everything that she'd said, but another part—a bigger part—refused to. She faced him, waiting for the onslaught that would certainly come.

"Come back inside."

She huffed. "Demanding."

"If you didn't want to be here, you'd have blurred away by now. Come inside. Please," Taylor added.

Her mind screamed for her to just leave. It would be easy. She only had to turn back around and take a step away. The next step would be easier, and so on, until she found herself safe and sound back inside her own home. When her eyes met with his, all she could see was the darkness, and it reflected so much more than just their current mood.

She glanced over her shoulder down the quiet street. When she glanced back towards her friend, he was standing so closely that she could feel his breath upon her cheeks. His expression, that had seemed so certain she would stay, now wavered into a worried tension that furrowed his brow. Could she walk away from him? Sure, she could… but would she?

"Lauren," he said this time in a gentler voice, "please."

She nodded, crossing her arms over her chest. He walked her

inside, making sure she sat on the couch before he spoke.

"I have no idea what crawled up your ass tonight, but we're going to get it all out on the floor now."

"Taylor—"

"No, you don't get to shout at me like that without following through. And don't even bother saying that this has only something to do with tonight. You've been like this for a while now," he pushed.

"I never used to be this irritable, I'll admit that, but a girl has got her limits, Taylor." She stood up, pacing the floor, trying to comb through her words. If he was going to actually listen to her, then she needed to hit the bullet points hard. "I'm not who I used to be. You saw what I went through, but seeing and being are two very different things. I just can't take being dominated or commanded like I don't have a mind of my own. Do you know how hard it was for me to come back to campus that first time after I changed? I knew it was a bad idea—that something bad would happen—and I was right."

Taylor stood silently with his lips clamped shut. He would wait until she finished, giving her the usual silent treatment, although this time seemed harder than usual. She turned her back on him, pacing again to steel herself to pull out the root of it.

"The only reason I went back was because of you. You're my best friend. I could have taken off and tossed my phone without a second thought. The Bellator in me pushed me to do just that. As you can see, I'm still here."

She raked her fingers through her hair. "Pretending to be what I'm not is extremely taxing and tiring. Add a sadistic mob trying to reel me into their way of life by making examples of innocent humans, and a psychotic bitch who knifed me, nothing has been easy. Everyone is just waiting for me to make a choice when it's already been taken out of my hands, don't you see?

"Quinn is trying to play mad scientist with my life source. Fallon would like me to disappear completely. Collin sees me as his next conquest." She rolled her eyes at that. "No one even sees me as Lauren anymore, other than you. You're the last drop of blood in this Bellator body. So you can imagine, when everything goes to shit and I can't take anymore that I'm more irritable. Especially with you. You're all I truly have left of a life that ended without my permission."

Her chest warmed as her throat clogged, and she struggled to catch her breath. All this emotion seemed to collect between her ribs causing further pressure. She wrapped her arms around her stomach as if to ease it. She tried breathing slowly and deeply, but to no avail. She laughed without humor. "I live in hell. Surrounded by beautiful things that will never be part of my life. If I disappeared, memories of me would fade, too. And maybe they should."

"What the fuck is that?" Taylor seethed. "You're supposed to be here. Don't give me the 'it's hard' bullshit. Of course it is. That's the entire point of living. It's not supposed to be easy."

Lauren could barely speak as her breaths became even shallower no matter how deeply she tried to breathe in. She couldn't even look at him as his voice resonated against the walls. "I'm not alive anymore."

"You are to me," he said, coming up behind her. "You are alive to me."

She felt his arms wrap tightly around her, still taught with agitation. She could hear what he wasn't saying. Anything was better

181

than nothing, and she was the 'anything' for him. She was his last drop of blood.

"Don't cry," he soothed as he held her tighter.

Lauren faced him in horror. "I can't. I physically can't do it!"

He peered down at her dry face, still managing to keep her within his arms. She stared at him, perplexed by his concern as he studied her like he always had. He took in every detail of her face like if he didn't, she'd be easily forgotten. Maybe that was the case.

"The only emotion you've shown is anger. Other than caring for innocent lives..."

"What are you getting at?" she asked.

"Two polar opposite emotions. Anger and love."

"Anger isn't the opposite of love, fear is. I'm not afraid of loving others," she replied.

"Your fear of being forgotten or fading away would. Fear that no one cared enough to get to know you. But you know that's not true. Your parents could never forget you, and neither could I."

Her voice trembled. "This is temporary. By May we'll be graduating and—"

His lips crushed hers, stopping the words he didn't want to hear. Pulling back after a moment, he said, "You can be so fucking depressing."

The shock of his actions had barely registered in her mind as her instincts took control. She pulled him closer, feeding on his loneliness as he worked to prove how alive she was.

*****

182

Lauren awoke with a jolt. She placed a hand upon her chest, but her heart was calmly beating. It had been a dream or a nightmare. Part of her was relieved, while the rest was tormented by the possibility. Had she felt this way for him all along? What did it say about her that she could willingly try for him?

Too tired to think any deeper about it, she lay back into the pillows, wriggling into a comfortable position. A warm arm clasped around her, tugging her into an equally warm body. Her eyes widened, recognizing the naked man in bed with her. Taylor snuggled into the back of her neck, sighing with ease.

Any possibility of her falling asleep had disappeared. Any possibility of what she thought happened the night before being a dream was gone. She had done the unthinkable. The inexcusable. Blurring the lines of their friendship with his feelings of abandonment only to fall into his bed. She was his rock, his no-matter-what-happened go-to girl. What would he think of her now?

"It's early. Go back to sleep," he whispered into her neck.

As if to protest for her, Links & Chains blared from her purse on the nightstand. She reached over to get the phone, hesitating when she saw her home phone number displayed. She sat up, looking around the room, noticing her clothes spread all over. She spent the night with her best friend, and her mom would know. She hit ignore on the call but quickly texted her mom that she was on her way home.

Lauren tossed her phone in her purse as she scrambled out of bed, using the blanket to cover herself. Finding her undergarments, she quickly tossed them on before crossing the room to grab her jeans. She could feel her backside radiating with heat and glanced over at Taylor sitting up, scratching the back of his head.

"Who called?"

"My mom," she said, leaning over the side of the couch to grab her shirt. "I've never not come home before..."

"Oh," he responded with a smirk. "Why are you covering up? I've already seen you."

Lauren could feel her face flush immensely at his words. He'd done more than just see her, but that wasn't the point. She wouldn't become his conquest simply because he needed it. She hadn't realized that she'd wanted more from him until now. Confronting him about what last night meant to her would be stupid, though.

She threw on her shirt before facing him. "I was cold."

Her phone started to go off again in her purse. Actually, putting an explanation to her parents into words was too much to ask for. She'd just brush it all off when she got home. She hit ignore on the phone and slid her feet into her boots.

"Do I have to bring you back now?"

"No," she blurted out quickly. "I'll tell her I was taking an early walk. I should probably work up a sweat so that it's believable."

Taylor laughed. "Nice choice of words. I'll take you back."

He slid out of bed, throwing on clothes and grabbing his keys to the car. She followed him out and into the car, all the while worrying about what was waiting for her back home. She pulled down the visor quickly, trying to comb her hair into an intentionally messy bun with her fingers.

"You're almost twenty-one. I doubt it's a huge deal," Taylor commented.

184

"I hope that you're right, but I doubt it."

Taylor shrugged, leaving her to think of endless possibilities awaiting her. Her anxiety only rose as she watched her mom step outside the front door as he pulled up to the curb. Her eyes were frosty as she came down the stairs. Lauren quickly unbuckled her seatbelt, grabbing the handle of the passenger door.

"Good luck," he said before driving off.

"Where have you been?" Mom asked.

Lauren readjusted the strap of the purse on her shoulder. "I'm sorry. I was out later than expected. I should have told you."

Her mom watched Taylor's vehicle disappear around the corner before shaking her head. "I'm still waiting for you to tell me. What happened?"

Being scolded in public sent a shiver through her that made her grit her teeth. She had put herself in this position, but it didn't change how much it sucked. She went into the house, knowing full well that she'd be followed. As the door shut behind them, her mom grabbed her arm, pulling Lauren to face her.

"I'm only going to ask you one last time."

"I lost track of time. I wasn't thinking," Lauren stated. "I'm sorry, Mom."

"Sorry doesn't cut it. That doesn't explain where you've been. It doesn't explain how your car made it home but you did not. Do you know how many thoughts went through my mind? Were you kidnapped? Were you hurt and in trouble? Do you know what type of panic you put me through? Not to mention your father."

Lauren looked towards the hallway but found it empty.

"Were you with Taylor the entire time?"

Lauren looked down at her intertwined fingers, but nodded.

"When I told you not to write him off, I certainly didn't mean for you to go off gallivanting with him all night long. I brought you up better than this."

"I didn't mean to make you mad. I'm sorry. Really, I am."

"I'm not mad, just disappointed," her mom said, walking towards the kitchen. "I think it would be a good idea for you to go back to school before your father gets back."

Lauren ran up to her room to find her bags still packed from the day before. She couldn't fathom the amount of worry she'd put her parents through or the fact that her mom had essentially just kicked her out. She packed her car in a foggy daze, trying to cope with what'd happened within a mere twenty-four hours.

Chapter Sixteen

Lauren pulled into the closest gas station to fill up the tank for the long drive back to campus. The morning was much colder than expected, even with her coat and scarf wrapped tightly around her neck. She tucked back into her car waiting for the signal that the car was filled. Her mind sought comfort after the tumultuous morning.

Her eyes were unfocused as she slowly opened them. A high-pitched beeping sounded nearby as she turned her head towards it. Gentle hands laid upon her fingers, applying light pressure.

"Lauren?"

She blinked as she tried to focus in on her mom's voice. Gentle kisses grazed her forehead and cheeks.

"Paul, she's awake," Claire said to Lauren's dad.

"Mom," she'd whispered, frightened. "I want to go home."

"Soon, okay?" Her mom glanced back as her father reached the other side of the bed.

"Hey there, kiddo," Dad greeted with equally gentle kisses upon her cheeks. "How do you feel?"

"Weird."

"Claire, will you let the nurse know she's awake," Dad asked. As her mom left the room, Dad leaned down and spoke softly. "You're allergic to bees, Lauren. Thank goodness you were with Taylor. What were you doing on Old Tavares' Property?"

Her eyes filled with tears. "I didn't mean to. Where's Taylor?"

"Home with his little brother. We told him to wait for his father to come home before trying to see you." His voice bordered between gratitude and concern.

187

"He helped me?" she asked as tears rolled down the side of her face. Her dad nodded. "What's wrong? Why are you crying, honey?"

"I want to see Taylor."

The gas pump dinged, pulling her out of her thoughts. She got out of the car, replacing the nozzle before climbing back inside her vehicle. If she was going to head back, she'd at least let him know. She texted Taylor quickly before throwing the car in drive.

The Bluetooth-enabled vehicle rang within a minute. "Taylor?"

"We're you serious about going back?"

"I was encouraged to by mom," she admitted.

"Screw that. Come here. There's nothing going on up there anyway."

"To be honest, going back doesn't sound that great, but I should. I have some unfinished business to tend to. Are you staying?" she asked.

"Dad will be back tomorrow. I should be here when I tell him."

"Will you see Marcus today?"

"If I said yes, would you believe me?" he asked, half-sighing.

"Of course, I would. Sort of."

He yawned into the line, not bothering to cover it. "I'm gonna grab a few more hours of sleep."

"Okay. See ya."

*****

It was mid-afternoon when she pulled into the parking lot. The campus appeared the same as always as she got out, pulling out her duffle. Even with her increased speed, unpacking the car was too much work. Her eyes were glazing over as she walked the pathway towards the dorm.

"Is this really the life you want to lead?"

Lauren looked up but found no one near her. She scanned her surroundings but saw nothing out of the ordinary. The sky was cloudy and gray, enhancing the creepy feeling. She took her time, checking her surroundings as she made it towards the dorm. Unfortunately, she didn't have her ID to get buzzed inside, and there was no one around.

She was effectively locked out of her sanctuary. Where could she go? Her skin was crawling at the thought of being watched by another Bellator. It was too cold outside for any students to be willingly hanging around.

"Come home to join your brothers and sisters."

Lauren's eyes scanned the campus, unable to find where the voice was coming from.

"It's not safe for you here. There's no future for you here."

"What do you know about a future? What do you know about me? Nothing!" Lauren shouted openly.

"Your future is with us. The lantern will guide you home, my dear."

"No!" she shouted. "No, I won't go with you!"

Lauren blurred as quickly as she could to the only place she could think of. It was in no way a safe haven, and was probably more dangerous than she realized, but her feet pushed her faster inside. She battled through the dangling cobwebs and debris, down the stairs until she found herself in the darkened lab.

She pulled open a few drawers, finding some syringes, which she grabbed. She then promptly hid beneath the desk. She waited and listened for any sounds of having been followed, but everything stayed eerily silent. As she sat listening, her mood got darker. The encounter with the voices left her irritable. Why wouldn't they just leave her alone?

The floorboards gently creaked above her head. Her eyes widened as her grip tightened around the syringes. She listened intently until she heard the steps creak, too. Would she be able to fight them off? Would it be better trying to run? She was fast, but what if they were, too?

"Keep it together, girl," Quinn said. "Don't come tumbling down just yet."

Lauren stuck out her head from under the lab table, watching Quinn turn on the light switch. He went to the cupboard, grabbing his goggles and lab coat. She crawled out, standing behind him while he closed the cupboard, patting its door.

"You talk to buildings?"

Quinn spun around quickly, only to find Lauren looking back dubiously at him. "What are you doing here?"

"I need some answers," she replied, placing the syringes on the table. "Any new developments with my DNA?"

"In less than twenty-four hours? Nothing huge, but it is what I expected. Why?"

Lauren sat on the stool, trying to shake off the adrenaline that coursed through her. "They want me, Quinn."

"Who? The Bellators? Well, it would make sense. They chose you for a reason," he replied, gazing back at the cage with the tiny mouse. "What do you feel for them in return?"

She hadn't thought about it. Becoming a Bellator had always had a negative association. What good could come out of being one, or rather, being like them? If she was honest with herself, she only felt fear when thinking about it. She was fearful of what they could do, and fearful of what she had become. Denying was easy but just as tiring as having patience with her circumstances.

"I feel nothing. I may be capable of awful things, but I know who I am. I'd never fit in with them, and that's a good thing."

"Have you been feeding?" he questioned.

She shook her head. "By the way, how'd you get mixed into all of this?"

"My uncle was a scientist. He's the reason for my interest in the subject at all. He came across a Bellator in his life. He tried to help but couldn't, and the afflicted ended up fading away. He taught me everything I know," he said. "And I know that if you don't feed regularly, you will not make it."

"I've made it this far without doing so. Not including the food poisoning thing."

"You're new to this way of life, Lauren. You're practically still sitting in wrapping paper like a gift," he commented. "The books you found in the library, did you think the information just appeared out of thin air?"

"You did it?"

Quinn focused on the microscope. "My uncle used to be a

professor here. They were his findings at the most basic level."

Lauren felt the need to question him further but held her tongue instead. She was much more concerned about the need to feed part. She wouldn't put her family and friends at risk if she could help it. How would she feed, though?

She wasn't hungry in the least, although she vividly remembered how the taste of Taylor's blood lingered on her tongue. It was the essence of life that satisfied the sickness within her. The sickness that wanted to take over her life. Her mind flashed to Taylor—how she had unintentionally hurt him physically only to lie with him hours later?

"You all right?" Quinn asked, staring at her curiously.

"Ummm... yeah, I'm fine. Thanks," she replied, averting her eyes towards the cage. "How's mousey doing?"

"He's fine, and don't name him like a pet. He isn't one."

She rolled her eyes, getting up from the stool. Maybe by now there would be someone going by the dorm so that she could get in. Some alone time was called for after the last day and a half she'd endured.

*****

After a long, well-deserved nap in the dorm, Lauren received a text from Hilary about a campus party. No excuse was good enough, leaving her only two options. One: just say no and put their friendship back on the rocks; or two: attend but slip out quietly after a little while. The latter seemed like the best option.

Allowing her hair to tumble down around her shoulders, she put on a small amount of makeup to appease her friends before heading out the door. Luckily, Max was the one throwing the party, which meant fresh new faces to meet. Not that she was looking to meet new people. Avoiding certain ones was mostly on her mind.

Max lived on the second floor, two below her and Taylor, which was so convenient. She wouldn't have to worry about being buzzed in and out. She knocked on the door a few times, but the music was loud enough to cover it. She sent a quick text to Gina that she was there, and the door swung open within minutes.

With a warm hug, she was welcomed inside. Gina was wearing her black skinny jeans with boots and cute beige tank top with a lace design around the edges. It made her feel better since she was pretty much wearing the same skinny jean ensemble but with a hunter green boat neck shirt.

"Glad you made it. Hilary is getting reinforcements with Tony," Gina advised.

"How are they doing?"

"It's pretty rocky," she whispered.

Lauren could imagine. Hilary had been pretty angry with her for ditching them, but coming in her hour of need had somehow made things okay. Even if the latter outcome had been horrific, she could appreciate the positive vibes that stemmed from it.

"Oh, and we're not doing the talent show anymore," Gina advised.

"Really?"

"Yeah. I think she got her kicks from that night," she said with a laugh. "And you're not a great singer."

Lauren laughed along with her. "Strangers were an easier crowd than anyone on this campus."

Gina grabbed her hand, tugging her towards the back of the crowded room. Lauren barely recognized any of the students around her. They easily fell into the sway of the music. She hadn't even noticed Hilary's return until she joined their dancing group.

She rocked a pair of torn jeans and a black short sleeve shirt with the sleeves ripped and entwined with burgundy ribbon. Of all her friends, Lauren admired Hilary's style the most—so outlandish and cool at the same time. For a while, the party disappeared. It was only the three of them dancing around to the vibes. Nothing else mattered.

"I need a drink," Hilary declared. "What do you guys want?"

"A beer, please," Gina replied before turning to Lauren.

"Nothing for me. I'm on a cleanse."

"A cleanse? That's cool. I'll join on Monday," Hilary laughed.

Gina smiled affectionately. "She'll forget after tonight," she commented sideways to Lauren.

Lauren nodded, knowing her friend all too well. Her intentions were honorable, but when it came to sticking to one thing for longer than a day or two, it would simply slip her mind. She was too flighty for long term plans like that. They continued swaying to the music until Hilary came back with beverages.

"Heads up. Collin and Gordon just got here."

Lauren's carefree mood slipped from her grasp as anxiety fell upon her shoulders. She glanced towards the door, trying to find an easy path of escape. Hilary stepped in her way, pushing her towards the side of the room.

"He'll head for the drinks first." Hilary glanced in that direction. "So, you two didn't hit it off?"

"Hilary, please. For once in your life, trust me to know my own heart. He isn't the one meant for me."

"I'm sorry," she said. "I'll go distract them."

Gina waited for her to make it to the table, striking up a conversation with them before making a path towards the door. Lauren kept her head down, making sure not to bump into people or step on anyone's feet until she could feel the cooler air as she entered the hallway.

"Believe it or not, I think Collin may actually be into you."

"What makes you say that?" Lauren asked as they walked into the stairwell.

"Max would kill me if he found out I said this, so keep it under wraps. But Collin hasn't been partying much at all. He's like in a daze, talking about a girl that he can't pin down. You've been seeing him, haven't you?"

"Nothing more than in passing. He sort of asked me out, but I didn't accept. I got sick and flaked," she admitted. "He's probably really pissed at me."

"He's not. At least talk to him. Let him know that you're not interested. That would be fair to him even if it sucks."

Lauren couldn't agree more, but she wasn't ready to pull the plug yet. She had no idea what her feelings were telling her. She'd only recognized that she was interested in Taylor, but that didn't mean a relationship. Or that *he* was interested. The biggest issue was her Bellator status. Collin would find out one way or another if he got closer, and she didn't want that, either.

"You're not into Collin, right?" Gina probed.

Lauren sighed, sitting on the steps. "He's nice."

"Glad you think so," Collin said, walking down the hallway. "Gina, can Lauren and I have a minute?"

Lauren stood up, startled at his presence. Gina, eyes wide with surprise, started towards the dorm room. Lauren flared her eyes at Gina, and Gina mouthed an apology with a gentle shrug. Collin gestured for Lauren to retake her seat back on steps.

"What happened to you the other night?"

"Can we not waste time with the small stuff? I'd rather we just be honest with each other up front," she said, ready to end this miserable situation as fast as possible.

Collin stood back in shock of her tone. "What do you mean?"

"What are you looking for from me?"

"Conversation. A few laughs?" he questioned. "Did you not want to hang out?"

"I did but… things are different now." She looked towards the empty hall, wishing for Gina to reemerge.

"Lauren, look at me." His eyes were focused directly upon hers as if he looked away she'd disappear. "Nothing is different between us, if you don't want it to be."

"It's not that easy."

"Of course, it is," he said, offering his palm to her. "Let's go back inside and have fun."

His proposition was easy, as was his smile. His eyes continued to bore into hers trying to keep her with him. Her friends would think they were together if she went in with him. Her social status worries dimmed the bigger issue she had regarding a potential relationship with him. Rumors could be hell and unstoppable.

She accepted his hand only to pull him into a hug. He welcomed it, relieving himself of a sigh that she wasn't meant to notice. Her actions were already set in motion before she could even think it through completely. She pulled out of the hug and took a step up the stairs. "Thanks, but I'm not going back. Have a good night, Collin."

Chapter Seventeen

The week blurred by as she concentrated on her studies. It took more effort for her to focus on her Historic Theatre course now that they were going to be performing the final. She kept her attention on the script within her hands, focusing on the paper that would accompany it. Better to pay attention to coursework than the fact that she had been lumped into the same performance as Collin.

He seemed to be much more vocal now in class, asking questions and offering his insights. It was almost like he was trying to stay in her head even if he had moved back to his original seat on the other side of the room. She couldn't be happier with the space, but it wouldn't help with the final.

Professor Klein encouraged the three groups of seven to exchange emails and set up preparation for the performance. Gloria had the best script out of the group, which left her as the producer. Lauren jumped at the opportunity to write up the presentation to keep from joining the actual performance. The lead, accepted by Collin, was a character trying to find himself through social status in the 1700s. The irony was that Collin was one of the most popular guys. Maybe he couldn't see that, though.

Lauren gathered up her belongings, placing the script within her binder. She made her way out of the building with excitement in her eyes. The long-awaited concert was tomorrow night at The Dome. She hadn't even known she'd been smiling until she realized someone was beside her.

"What?" Lauren asked.

"I didn't say anything," Fallon replied.

198

"What do you want?"

"To be rich? Oh, you mean, from you," Fallon smirked. "Checking in for Quinn."

Lauren rolled her eyes at that. "Nothing has changed."

"Have you been feeding?"

"Is that all you're worried about? I'm not, so don't," she replied.

"You know what will happen if you don't. Not that I care."

"Next question," Lauren pushed.

"That's it."

Lauren stopped to look her straight in the eye. "What the hell is that? Quinn doesn't stop at just one question."

"What's the point in going on if you don't feed? Again, not that I care. In fact, I'm pretty glad to hear it."

"You bitch."

Fallon laughed carelessly. "Temper, temper. I'm only applauding you for doing what you say. How many times have you said you didn't want to hurt anyone? And look at you… keeping your word."

Lauren stalked off, feeling her restraint with the girl slowly weaken.

"Poor Taylor, though," Fallon continued in the distance. "We both know how this ends for you, but does he?"

Fighting the urge to remove all of Fallon's teeth, Lauren blurred away to her room. Taylor was out, leaving her the quiet space she needed to write her presentation. She attempted several paragraphs' worth but couldn't get Fallon off her mind. She was so lucky that the girl wasn't in her group. It didn't help change how annoying she could be, though.

Her inbox pinged with a new email as she worked on the paper. It was from Collin, offering suggestions to make the paper easier to finish and asking some questions. The tone was one of urgency to respond. As much as she appreciated it, she was slightly annoyed. She'd just seen him. What could possibly be so important that it needed to be addressed right now?

Lauren grabbed her phone and dialed her carefree roommate. "Hilary, do you have a second?"

"For you, I have sixty," she laughed.

"Why would you think that Collin and I would be a couple?"

"Uh-oh, why?"

"You first," Lauren said.

"Well, he had been complaining of the airhead girls who surround him. He said it was easy pickings, which, you know, grossed me out and totally infuriated me. I told him that if he actually found a nice chick, maybe he'd enjoy the challenge and learn more about himself. That's when he mentioned you."

Lauren sat back in her seat. He thought she was nice. And also thought of her as smart instead of an airhead. He had been trying to get to know her, and she'd done nothing but put him off. She knew she was definitely a challenge, relationship-wise. Still, neither Hilary nor Collin knew what she'd become.

"Did something happen?" Hilary asked. "You looked so frightened when he showed up at the party."

"No, not with him," she said. "I'm having a hard time opening up at all. And maybe it's a sign that I shouldn't be trying."

"Maybe he's your challenge, too? Would you be willing to try to date him? No promises or commitments? Let him know your terms. Maybe it would take the pressure off," Hilary suggested.

"Eh. I'm gonna let you go, but thanks."

"You're welcome. See you," Hilary said.

Lauren stared at her computer screen with the email demanding her response. She began to respond civilly, accepting his suggestions on certain parts and answering his questions. Her last sentence was to thank him for the extra information. It was the best she could do to be nice.

Taylor came into the room, dripping sweat from the gym. He grabbed a change of clothes and went to the shower. She made a point of trying not to ogle him when he was around. Although they'd been together more intimately than she thought possible, things could get weird if she treated him more differently than normal.

She wasn't ignorant to the calming effect he was now producing when around, or to the fact that she couldn't really look him in the eye anymore. It was as though he could see her more clearly now than he ever could before. She could actually feel her face flush when he'd stare at her like he always had.

While he was out of the room, she rushed into her comfortable, plaid sleeping pants and t-shirt. She closed her laptop, getting into bed with her back towards the door. The sound of the door closing behind her was easily ignorable. She sighed into the pillows doing her best to push out all of her thoughts for the evening.

That was when the covers slid down her arm and bodily heat warmed her back. The smell of his body wash assaulted her senses, leaving no question as to whom her bedmate was. He snuggled into her neck, wrapping his arm around her in a comfortable exhale.

"The beds suck on campus," he complained.

"They can't all be plush, full sized beds."

Taylor pushed against her back, forcing her to move forward. She grasped the edge of the mattress instinctively protecting herself. "Maybe this isn't the best idea," she said.

"Kicking me out of your bed?"

"Either I kick you out, or I fall out," she admitted.

His grip tightened, pulling her further back into his chest. "Better?"

Lauren rolled over, turning to face him in the darkness of the room. The words she wanted to say were on the tip of her tongue, begging to be released from her mind. His close proximity was only making it harder to keep her thoughts to herself. "I'm pretty tired..."

He sat up for a moment in silence. She couldn't be sure what he was thinking but knew her mind was uncontrollably skittering to thoughts of their first time together. As much as she had enjoyed it, she had to keep her distance from him in that aspect. She needed to be strong for him; and more importantly, she needed to be strong for herself.

The bed rose as he slid out of it, leaving his scent behind to torment her for the rest of the night. She laid her head down on the pillow, staring up at the ceiling, wishing for strength that she wasn't sure she had.

*****

"Are you ready for tonight?" Taylor asked.

Lauren nodded while they stopped at the deli for a snack. He grabbed a Saran-wrapped sandwich with a bag of chips with a soda. She waited by the door while he paid at the register. They emerged into the chilly air, walking the path towards the parking lot.

"Can I ask you something without you gettin' pissed?"

Lauren tensed at his words but nodded again.

"You're not hungry at all?"

"No," she responded. "I'm fine, Taylor."

"I could spare a bit, you know."

Lauren hid how enticing that sounded, but she refused to be a monster. She wouldn't feed on anyone, especially her best friend. She closed her eyes trying to gain control of her thoughts. "I'm okay."

"Shed this shell and come home," a strange voice beckoned.

"What?" she asked, stopping on the path.

"I didn't say anything," Taylor replied.

"Come home now," the voice beckoned with sternness.

Her eyes widened, realizing the danger this posed for Taylor as much as it did for her. She looked towards her friend, reaching out for his hand. She'd drag him away if she had to. Taylor accepted, stepping closer to her side. "What is it?"

"Let's get going."

His body tensed up in reaction to hers as they made their way quickly toward his car. He wasted no time, throwing the car in drive, taking off northbound towards the highway. The farther he went, the less anxiety she felt until she weakly sank into the seat.

"You all right?"

"I'm sorry. I should have told you," she said.

"Told me what?"

"The Bellators have been calling to me. Wanting me to leave with them," she admitted. "It's getting worse."

"Is that what just happened?" he asked, the anger easily sparking in his eyes.

"They want me to go home to them."

Taylor checked the rearview mirror and the cars surrounding them. "Do you think they're following us?"

"I don't know. Maybe? Maybe not. I mean, they know that I stay on campus."

"You don't belong with them. They don't know anything about you," he stated sternly. "Right? You don't want to go with them, do you?"

"Of course not. This is where I want to stay. Right here, where I can be happy surrounded by my friends and family. Going to see Links & Chains to have a memorable night with you. What more could I ask for?"

Taylor glanced in the mirror one last time. Lauren wanted nothing more than to ignore the Bellator situation for one night. At least for tonight. "Can we pretend that it hadn't happened? Please?"

"You can't even defend yourself," he said.

"I won't have to. Everything will be okay."

He grumbled beneath his breath but didn't reply. She checked her purse, confirming the concert tickets were safely inside before staring out the passenger window. Trees sprinkled the highway giving way to open farmland before the trees emerged again for some of the smaller suburban towns. Soon, those small towns would give way to the sprawling city where The Dome resided.

She couldn't believe the awesome seating he'd managed to snag for the show. It was lower level right by the stage on the aisle with no worries of someone to get in their line of view. The entire arena could easily sit twenty thousand people, and as it began to fill with fellow fans, she thought it possible it might be filled to capacity tonight.

Taylor sat beside her tensely, shoulders bunched up with his eyes scanning the crowd around them. She leaned into his side, tugging lightly on the sleeve of his shirt. He leaned into her marginally, but the gesture forced him to sit back into the seat completely.

"I've got a secret," she whispered.

"Another one?"

Lauren gave him a shy smile. "Tonight, I'm human."

"That's not how it works—"

"I'm going to be girly and annoying and ask for you to get me things," she said, cutting him off.

"Great," he replied sarcastically.

She giggled beside him. "It will be."

The opening band appeared on stage with more enthusiasm than she thought could be packed into thirty minutes. The music was upbeat with techno vibes intertwined with an eighties rock theme. It was almost impossible for her to not fall in love with them. She'd already put them in her phone to look up when she got back to campus.

When the lights came back on, Lauren was thrilled and ready for more. She sat back down in her seat, as anticipation built for her favorite band. Taylor stayed quietly beside her, merely watching the show without much care.

"Are you at least going to stand for them?"

"Maybe," he replied. "How are you so buoyant tonight?"

Lauren pushed her hair back from her face. "Why aren't you? You bought the tickets for this."

"Obviously, it's a good band. I just can't shake it off."

"I'm right here, Taylor," she said, gesturing towards herself. "What more can I do?"

He shook his head, pulling out his phone. "Nothing."

The lights slowly began to dim as the crowd roared with excitement. Lauren stood up, ignoring Taylor's moodiness, trying to live in the moment.

Hunter emerged in the foggy mist, whispering the beginning lyrics to the first hit single before the fireworks blasted in the background. It was the most spectacular moment she was certain couldn't be felt again. She bounced on the balls of her feet to the beat.

It wasn't until she heard the familiar strumming of the acoustic guitar that her heart began to beat faster. Her body already knew what was coming, making it impossible for her to stay calm. That's when Hunter's lips grazed the microphone, focusing her eyes on the detailed gesture.

"How many of you have seen us live before?"

The crowd screamed aloud in reply, waving arms in the air.

"That's awesome. Thank you," he replied. "How about the first timers?"

Another round of screamers flooded the air causing a huge grin to grace his face.

"Well, it's about time you showed up!" Hunter laughed. "No, seriously, thank you for coming out tonight. You're all beautiful!"

Hunter strummed a few chords of his guitar as the drums began to lightly play behind him. His wide smile transformed into a Cheshire cat grin. "This is one of my favorite songs. So if you're here with your best friend, your lover, your soul mate, take them by the hand and sing along with me."

His hands came to life as his voice sounded over the speakers. It was Illuminated Lovers. She knew every word by heart, and part of her felt that her heart was singing louder than the rest of the crowd. As warmth radiated against her side, she felt Taylor's fingers gently intertwine with hers. She couldn't see his eyes in the dark, only the reflection of the lights from the stage.

The tempo began to pick up with the drummer leading the way until his drum solo. The stage darkened with a beaming light shining on the drum set. When the lights came back up, Hunter emerged from the side with his electric guitar around his neck. The drummer led right back into the bridge of the song as Hunter sang aloud to the upbeat song.

Lauren swayed to the music as her spirits lifted. She couldn't imagine being anywhere else as the grip of her hand tightened within Taylor's. She didn't even question him when their eyes met. It was a gravitational pull that bonded them into one.

His kiss was tender as he embraced her, continuing to sway slowly to the music. With the darkness surrounding them, having only temporary moments of flashes from the show, it seemed they were the only ones in the entire arena. For the rest of the show, she stayed tucked within his arms.

The drive back towards campus was comfortable with the radio playing in the background. Their hands remained entwined as he drove with a carefree energy that lightened the atmosphere in the vehicle. She found her lips stuck in a permanent smile that was reflected right back to her.

Her phone vibrated in the purse at her feet. Knowing it was only a text message, she ignored it, watching the dark shadows of the trees pass by in a blur. Part of her didn't want to go back to campus, and with every lamppost, she knew they were getting closer by the minute.

"What's wrong?"

"Nothing, why?" she asked.

He gripped her hand gently. "Tensing up."

"I'm not ready to go back. I wanna stay like this for a while longer."

"What's the difference?" he asked. "Tonight, you're human."

Lauren laughed aloud at his reminder. "This is true. Do we have any chocolate pudding left in the room?"

"I have one left, and human or not, you get none."

She nodded in agreement, having no plans of getting sick again. The simple plans ahead sounded like just what she needed. Her energy levels were low after a long day and the concert, but the unexpected still loomed. Would she hear from the Bellators again tonight?

Taylor pulled into the parking lot on campus. As she stepped out, her eyes scanned her surroundings, unsure of what to expect. She wasn't imagining that Taylor felt the same way as he, too, came to her side, walking up the main path towards the dorm. When they made it safely into the lobby of the dorm, both sighed in relief.

"At least I keep things interesting, right?"

"That's one way to put it," he said, placing a hand on her lower back. "Come on. It's late."

Lauren went up the stairs ahead of him, feeling the long day begin to weigh on her shoulders. It wasn't until they were going up the second flight of stairs that she stopped in her tracks, stunned. At the landing stood Tony and Collin. She tucked her hair behind her ears, paying extra attention at her steps.

"Oh, man, Taylor, you missed the game tonight," Tony said. "Oklahoma played Texas into overtime."

"It was pretty awesome. I lost too much, though," Collin admitted.

Taylor nodded. "That sucks. When's Texas play again?"

"Monday night. They're going up against Illinois," Tony said. "I thought you'd be over at Max's tonight."

"Nah, I got tickets to a concert. We're just getting back," Taylor replied, nodding in her direction.

"Who'd you see?" Collin asked her directly.

"Links & Chains," she said. "They put on a great show."

Tony covered his mouth to hide his yawn. "I'm beat. I'll see you guys later."

"Yeah, me too," Taylor said, continuing towards the next set of stairs. He glanced back noticing Lauren hadn't followed. "You coming?"

Lauren noticed Collin's confused expression at the request.

Clearly, he hadn't suspected that she'd be staying with Taylor overnight. And as his eyes widened, she decided to make light of the situation. "In a second," she said to Taylor.

When her eyes locked with Collin's, she wasn't sure what to say. He wasn't making any attempt to say anything, either, extending the awkward silence that much more. She thought of a bunch different ways to begin, but they all seemed to be a waste of breath.

"So…"

"You're staying the night. Here." His statement was clear with its intent.

"Yes," she said clearly, without hesitation. "It's not a big deal."

"Is something going on between you two? I mean, I thought you were just friends."

"He's my best friend. What's this really about, Collin?"

"Nothing," he said, starting to walk away from her towards the stairs.

"I thought *we* agreed to just be friends," she said.

"What are you even talking about? There was no agreement," Collin said. "I asked you out, and you no-showed. I confront you on it, and you don't commit to anything."

Lauren blinked in a stunned silence. What was she supposed to say? Everything he said was true. She couldn't help that she was interested in someone else… and that someone was waiting upstairs for her.

"I'm not ready to be in a serious relationship right now. It's no secret—go ahead and ask Hilary or Gina or even Tony. You and I have been getting to know each other, but I'm not going to just jump into something because I've been asked. Please understand that this isn't personal against you," she admitted. "I'd rather know what I'm getting myself into before committing to anything. That's who I am."

Lauren went up the stairs, leaving Collin with something to think about. She did want to sustain a civil relationship with him, especially while they were dealing with the upcoming final. She took a few deep breaths until she felt calm enough to walk inside the room.

Taylor was sitting on the edge of his bed with the TV remote lying beside him. When she entered the room, he turned the volume down. She placed her purse on her desk before taking a seat on her own bed. He cleared his throat, and she closed her eyes, hoping his only complaint was the lack of his favorite dessert.

"We should talk," he began. "This is… important."

"I don't think I can handle another conversation tonight, Taylor."

"It's not going to take long. Look, I know Collin is into you, and if you want to date him or whatever, then you should," he said.

"What?" she asked shocked. "Where is this coming from? I've never once—"

"I'm an all or nothing man, Lauren. I like to have a good time, but I'm not what you may think I am," he interrupted. "I'm used to having nothing, and I like it that way."

Her chest wanted to cave in. She opened her mouth, but only air escaped like a swift kick had knocked her in the ribs without her seeing it, but she had certainly felt the impact. Seeing her reaction, he went over, sitting beside her. He placed his hand gently upon hers.

"You're an all type of woman, Lauren. What we did, what we

shared together, will always mean something to me. Tonight, being with you—"

"Stop."

"No, I need you to listen to me," he said, looking her straight in the eyes. "We crossed a line that we shouldn't have; that was my fault. I want you to be happy, and that won't happen with me."

"Please stop talking," she begged, refusing to look at him any longer. The initial impact was wearing off, leaving tight pressure and pain in her chest. Her eyes frantically searched the room for her purse. She should leave.

The pain began to ricochet within her chest causing her to inhale deeply as she stood up. Her hand flashed to the desk. Grabbing up her purse, she headed for the door. She didn't even get the chance to open it before he was hot on her trail.

"Lauren, no," he said. "Don't leave."

She pulled it open anyway, ignoring his request. Her actions and her thoughts were in sync. It was her mouth that she couldn't depend on. Unexpectedly, the door shut in front of her face with the force of his hand. He slid in between her and the door, forcing her to look him in the eyes. Whatever he saw in her eyes encouraged him to grab her by the shoulders. "Lauren, stay with me."

"I have," she whispered. "I've stayed, but I can't anymore."

"Were you expecting something else? That this would become—"

"I haven't been honest with you," she spoke certainly. Facts were facts. He was honest with her, and it was the least she could do in return. "My being part of your life is temporary. It was my own weakness that I've stayed this long."

"What the fuck are you talking about?"

"Bellators aren't that different from humans, after all. Humans need food to survive…" she said, letting the empty space fill in the rest.

His dark eyes seemed impossibly darker. "When were you going to tell me that? Were you ever planning to? Or were you just going to disappear?"

Lauren blinked numbly. "I'd hope that you'd know me better than that by now. That after all these years together, you'd know that I could never do to you what *she did*. For you to see what we've become because of *her actions*. But I'm starting to realize how wrong I've been about quite a few things. I'd like to be alone now, so please move."

The words came across strongly even in the strange voice that came from her throat. Realization began to slap her in the face all at once. Just by sticking close to him and the school, she'd never be able to break away from the human world. She was a Bellator; there was no hiding from the existence that she was forced into.

Taylor stepped aside, shocked, allowing her enough space to open the door to exit. As she stepped through, he grabbed her arm weakly. "I can't lose you, too."

The frustration was still locked in his expression, but the fear he usually suppressed was blatant in his eyes. She'd always succumbed to his will when he asked her for things. Having him actually say the words aloud cut her deeper than her own pain of rejection. His pain was something that he carried around every day, and she wanted nothing more than to ease it. She'd spent every chance she could to support him since the day his mother walked out, but after tonight, what could she really do? She was only a body that he was used to having around. He didn't truly care like she did for him.

"Then don't let *me* go," she whispered softly to herself as she walked down the hallway.

Chapter Eighteen

The veins in her eyes appeared black again with strain. She could only hope that the eyeliner and mascara would keep it from being easily noticed. The girls hadn't minded her spending the night the last few days. It wasn't a permanent fix, just a temporary state until she could figure out her next move.

Sleep was a necessary evil. Her mind fluttered through the painful memories of the night she left Taylor like she'd been cursed. The only reprieve was a dream. She dreamt of being surrounded by monsters only to find herself staring one in the mirror. There was no chance of further sleep after that.

Instead, Lauren worked on the presentation for the final, finishing it early enough to send to her group for approval. She'd received positive reviews from everyone except one. Collin hadn't bothered to reply at all.

Regardless of her minor break from classes after her attack and change, she'd managed to keep up her grades. Her thoughts seemed to scatter much easier now that she wasn't around her friends that much. Even while living with Hilary and Gina, Taylor had been her anchor. They'd weathered all the storms together. Now she was drifting off with no real course ahead.

Her phone vibrated against the table. She flipped to the message; it was from Quinn.

Have you fed?

She texted back a quick 'no' and went back to her work. She was shocked when her phone began to ring. She didn't bother looking at the display.

"What?"

"When was the last time you fed?"

"When I had food poisoning," she replied factually.

"You won't last much longer if you don't feed, Lauren. Even a few drops every once in a while would be better than this."

"Why should it matter?"

"Are you ready to die now?" Quinn asked harshly. "Because that's what will happen."

"I don't want to exist like this."

"Wallowing in self-pity won't get you anywhere. Just have some patience, all right?" Quinn said. "I've been working on something to help. It's not a cure but it's... something."

"That's reassuring. You have *something*," she repeated sarcastically.

"Come to the lab, and you'll see what I mean."

She hung up with a huff. It was already beginning to get dark, and it was only about five in the evening. Winter was going to be brutal this year. She was more certain of that than anything else.

Lauren grabbed her coat, slinging her purse over her shoulder before heading outside. The frost on the sidewalk was still present, but the nip in the air made it clear that the actual snowfall would soon be arriving. She made the quick trip around the campus and inside the building.

Quinn was hovering over a microscope when she went into the lab. He wrote down a few notes before acknowledging her. He waved her over towards the cage holding the little gray mouse. The cage appeared empty like it usually did until he lifted the opening at the top and dropped in a small slice of orange. The mouse squeaked as it ran towards the fruit, nibbling at it in haste.

"He can't eat that without getting sick," she complained aloud.

"Shhh… just watch."

The mouse devoured his snack, licking his paws and then using his wet paws to clean his face. He stared up towards the opening waiting for another slice to drop down. Quinn shook his head, closing the lid, which caused the mouse to retreat back into his hidden space.

"What'd you do?" she asked.

"I injected the fruit with two drops of human blood. He eats it with no knowledge and doesn't get sick. I've recreated that into a pill form for you."

"Food is the last thing on my mind right now."

"Participating in a world that doesn't know that you exist is difficult. I get that. Why not at least make it easier to conceal yourself?" he questioned.

"The Bellators know who I am—"

"This isn't for them. This is for humans and for you. You won't feed, otherwise. This will keep you healthy," Quinn interrupted. "This is part one of the something I've been working on."

"I'm not drinking your blood, Quinn," she said stubbornly. "What's the real reason why you're fighting for me?"

"There is a cure. There has to be. If you think about the world, it's made up of opposites. If there is an illness then there is a cure. It just hasn't been figured out yet." He went over to the book sitting beside the microscope, pointing out a specific diagram. "We already know the differences from experience between human and Bellator DNA; however, your Bellator DNA is different. It reacts uniquely, only following the bare basics of what it should."

"Is this part two?"

"If I can manipulate the right element in your DNA, this could be bigger than we both thought possible. It might not be a cure, but it could be…. something," he said. "And while I'm trying to figure this out, you should at least do your part." Quinn nodded toward a white bottle on the counter.

Lauren picked it up, unscrewing the child protective cap, and took a quick glance inside. It was filled with tiny, black-colored gel capsules. She quickly screwed the top back on and set the bottle down on the counter. "I'm not drinking your blood."

"It will stay fresh with anticoagulant. There's only two drops per capsule and enough for two weeks' worth of human food consumption," he stated while staring in the microscope. "And it's not mine."

Her eyebrows scrunched up in confusion. "Not yours? Then whose?"

Quinn remained silent. Certainly Fallon wasn't volunteering, but who else would be willing…

Her eyes widened with realization. "Taylor? He did this?"

"I didn't say anything."

Lauren couldn't find the words to express her emotions. Anger was prominently at the top of the list, but it usually was. Or it had been before that night…

She had to thank him for his gesture, whether she wanted to or not. She had to mean the words she said, but facing him would be out of the question. There was no way she'd be prepared to stare into those dark chocolate eyes, listening to his vulgar vocabulary and what not.

"Did he tell you about the visitors?"

Quinn nodded. "They won't stop until they get you back. And if my suspicions are right, we know why."

*****

Lauren waited until she was tucked safely into her makeshift bed before taking on the task of reaching out to Taylor. This way, she was already comfortable in her pajamas, she was tired enough to sleep and surrounded by her girlfriends who seemed really glad to have her back. She sank into the pillows, pulling up his contact information.

Thank you for offering your blood. Quinn didn't say anything, but you're the only one who would do that. I'm very appreciative.

His response came within seconds. *Want to test it out?*

She hadn't actually thought of consuming the contents of the bottle. Admitting that to him would set off something she wasn't prepared for. Instead, she texted back a simple response. *Sure, maybe tomorrow or something.*

Taylor texted back. *Breakfast?*

Lauren wasn't in any rush, leaving it vague. *Eh, probably not. Going to sleep. Ttyl.*

She promptly turned her phone to silent, setting the alarm for the morning, and rolled over. She closed her eyes and tried her best to think pleasant things like puppies and kittens playing together. She'd seen plenty of videos online. After a few minutes, she realized that her body wasn't ready no matter how much she wanted it to be.

She picked up her phone to watch one of the videos when she noticed a longer response from her friend.

Stop dodging me. Breakfast in the morning it is. Sleep well.

Lauren sat up abruptly. She wanted to reply. She wanted to tell him to take a hike. Her instincts told her that she was overreacting because she was still upset about the last time they'd seen each other. It didn't change that she still didn't want to see him.

She got out of bed, quietly pacing the floor, seeing that Hilary was already passed out. Her nerves were bouncing around within. Any chance of sleep now had evaporated. Then Gina walked into the room, catching her mid-pace.

"You okay?"

Lauren nodded. "I'm more awake than I should be."

Gina dropped off her purse and bag on the desk. "I think that midterm is worse than finals."

"They equal out unless you bomb one or the other," Lauren said, trying to sit still on the edge of her bed.

"I think you're going off," Gina commented, pointing to her phone.

The cell phone was lit up with music notes floating across the screen. She reached over to answer when it hung up. It was from Quinn, which was strange; she'd just seen him a few hours ago. She called back but received no answer.

She threw her hair up into a messy bun and changed into warmer clothes. She grabbed her coat and headed for the door.

"Who was that?"

"Quinn. I have to go," Lauren said as she ran out the door.

She dialed his number again but still received no answer. Maybe it was the anxiety from dealing with Taylor, but she couldn't help the feeling that something was wrong. And the fact that he wasn't answering only made it worse. She flew down the stairs, blurring through the lobby until she was outside.

Lauren gave it one last dial and the call went straight to voicemail. Her back stiffened as she raced towards the old science building. She lost her breath as she saw the smoke rising and the flames screaming from every window. As she got closer, she couldn't see anyone outside. No one had even noticed.

Smoke was coming out the entrance she usually used, but there were no flames near it. She went inside noting how utterly destroyed everything looked. The usual path that was clear of debris was missing. Floorboards from the second floor had come down even more, making it almost impossible for her to get around. The smoke was almost blinding, but she used her shirt to cover her mouth as she made her way through to the stairs.

"Help!" a voice called from below.

The ever-rickety steps for once weren't the scariest part of going into the basement level. Pushing open the lab door, she began to cough uncontrollably. The lab tables were toppled over, stools smashed into burning wood pieces and part of the first floor had collapsed.

"Quinn?!" she coughed.

"Lauren!" he choked. "Over here."

The rubble surrounding the cupboard was made up of the wooden floorboards from above, ceiling matter and paint chips. She tried to lift some of the pieces, but they were too heavy. She found his legs pinned between the cupboard and ceiling with some pieces burning near where his head was.

"Are you okay?" she asked, trying to find a way to get him out without being burned.

"Not really. This thing," he gestured to the heavier piece of floorboard, "is on my shins."

The fire near his head began to catch on some of the papers scattered on the floor. She tried to lift up the floorboard again but only moved it a fraction of a centimeter. What could she use to help? She searched nearby for anything to use as leverage just as Fallon came through the door.

"Help me move this," Lauren shouted.

The two girls grabbed the edge of the board, pushing it over enough that Quinn could sit up and tuck his knees to his chest before they let it go. Fallon reached down, helping him stand up. Lauren took in how quickly the room was beginning to fill with more smoke as the fire spread in the basement level.

"We have to get out of here," she said.

"Not without my research," Quinn said. "Fallon, the portfolios."

Quinn started to grab up some of the vials, placing them in his backpack. Lauren grabbed what she could, helping to fill the backpack with everything she got her hands on. When that was full, she helped Fallon gather up the stacks of portfolios.

"Let's go," Fallon said, leading the way out.

Lauren carried what she could manage as Quinn followed them up the stairs. The main level was worse than before. More of the ceiling had come down, and the floorboards were weakening beneath their feet. The room was almost completely black with smoke as they made their way through, coughing and choking.

When they emerged into the cold, fresh air, she was grateful that she'd shown up. They carried the contents to Quinn's car for safe keeping. Lauren laid her head against the side of the vehicle, trying to catch her breath. It tasted wrong on her tongue, but that was to be expected.

"What happened?" Fallon coughed out.

"Don't know for sure. I was working with her DNA, and then I heard all this noise stomping around. I didn't get a chance to check before the ceiling came down on me," Quinn explained.

"Did we get all your research?" Fallon asked.

"Most of it. I'm not too worried about the few papers left." He placed his hand on the backpack. "These are irreplaceable."

Lauren glanced back at the building as the fire took hold of the second floor with new life. She was only too happy to be far away from that mess. She took in Quinn and Fallon, glad that they made it out alive and in one piece, although Quinn was definitely bruised up. That's when someone else clicked in her mind.

"The mouse!" Lauren shouted through shock. "We left him."

"It's just a mouse. We can use another," Fallon replied.

"All lives matter!" Lauren screamed as she shoved Fallon back in anger. Lauren blurred back inside the building. The main level was now a pure black obstacle course she was even less prepared for. She tried to remember what had been where but couldn't as she tripped and stumbled over ceiling fragments on the floor. There was no way she'd have found the stairs except by pure luck.

She scampered down the steps, headed right into the lab where the fire was coming to full fore. The heat was so intense that her eyes became dry no matter how much she blinked. The plus was the light that the fire gave off. She could see the cage and grabbed one of the lab coats, wrapping it around her hands for protection. She didn't have to heart to check on the mouse until she knew they were both safe.

Lauren made her way out of the lab and up the stairs. As she reached the top, one of the stairs weakened completely, sending her to the ground, rattling the cage as it crashed into the stairs. Squeaks sounded in response. She grabbed the wooden rail for support, but it bowed with the tension.

As she leveraged her weight on her good leg, she tried to crawl up, pulling herself level. The pain in her leg was unmistakable, but she couldn't stop now. She was already so close. She tugged herself up, wrapping her hand with the lab coat again. She maneuvered her way with the cage through the main level, hearing squeaks every time she tripped over something, which was often. The opening to outside was barely noticeable as she took a step out, only for her injured leg to give out from under her.

She and the cage went tumbling down to the sidewalk. She coughed repeatedly, throwing up slightly. The mouse squeaked in protest of being dropped so much. She could only be happy that she'd rescued it from the inferno inside. The pleasure of having her cheek rest against the moist pathway would do nothing to take away the attention of the pain shooting through her leg.

Pulling herself up into a sitting position, she didn't have to pull up the leg of her jeans to see that this was worse than she thought.

Spots of her life force were peeking through the fabric and sticking to the ground beneath her. She looked towards the parking lot where she'd run from Quinn and Fallon but was unable to see them from where she sat.

"Quinn!" she yelled. After a few seconds of only sounds from the burning building, she tried again. "Qui—!"

*****

Lauren cried out as she was abruptly dropped onto the floor. A foreign object had been forced into her mouth making speaking impossible. She couldn't take too many deep breaths or she'd choke and start coughing, which only made it harder to breathe. She was long past afraid and had now entered petrified. Where the hell was she?

"Be careful with her, Elijah. She's already broken," a familiar female voice commented.

"It's her own fault."

"All the same, be careful with her," she said. "Are you hungry?"

"Always. Let me drop off the cargo first."

Lauren felt the hard ground disappear from beneath her as strong arms lifted her up. The cloth tied so tightly over her eyes prevented her from knowing exactly where she was. Not that she couldn't guess. Not that she wanted to.

She was put down this time in a gentler fashion onto a softer surface. Elijah's hand grabbed the ankle of her injured leg, tugging the fabric up.

"Damn," he said before pulling the fabric back down.

"Elijah," another familiar voice beckoned from somewhere close. "Dinner is waiting."

"Yes, sir." She could feel Elijah's presence back away from her. "Her left leg was damaged prior to my getting her back."

"Of course it was. I don't doubt you." His voice was stern with a hint of sarcasm. "And you..."

The raspiness echoed off of his stern voice, causing goose bumps to rise upon her skin. Part of her was glad that she couldn't see him. It would take the power away from how important he felt. At least that was what she was hoping was the case.

"You could have joined us when we offered. Now the choice is no longer yours," he said with a voice that was calm and deadly serious. "Someone has been waiting to meet you."

The End

About The Author

M. L. Newman is an independent writer who lives in rural Connecticut with her wonderful husband. She is a member of the RWA. She has a bachelor's degree in Social Sciences from Marist College. She is active in community theatre and has played characters ranging from Brigitta Von Trapp in The Sound of Music to Ms. Hannigan in Annie which has inspired the many fun aspects and personalities for the characters in her romance novels.

M. L. Newman is currently hard at work on the sequel to *The Fade Away Series*, but she'd love connecting with you on her Facebook page https://www.facebook.com/pages/M-L-Newman/508027985916037 and on Twitter https://twitter.com/MLNewman1

Looking for exclusive content and more?
Visit www.mlnewmanauthor.com